Robert's Requiem

By Jon Patten

ISBN-13: 978-0-578-24232-3

For Chris.

1

Atlas Mironoff stood in the center of his new warehouse and struck a pose reminiscent of Benito Mussolini or Saddam Hussein. His eyes scanned across the expanse of the warehouse, taking in what he'd accomplished in less than a week.

Just four days ago he opened the door to this vast empty building and saw nothing but potential. He knew it would be perfect. With some minor work, he could bring industrial organization and volume to his side business, incalculably raising the return he'd receive on what was going to become his prime operation.

One-hundred eighty-thousand square feet of opportunity, of growth, of efficiency in an inefficient, but highly lucrative, business.

And here he was, six days later, his imposing figure front and center of the warehouse; his cold, expressionless face watching dozens of employees bustling about in torrents of activity.

To his left, chain-link fencing sectioned off a full third of the warehouse was sectioned off, with open floor behind the fencing. Next to it, four rows of small plywood boxes, each about eight by 10 feet.

Plywood walls completely closed off the final third.

Perfect. Mironoff blushed, he couldn't help himself. Looking at this space, and picturing his future wealth, was too exciting. He raised his hand and ran his thick fingers across the stubble of black hair sprouting on his head. His left hand slid across an eye, making sure no one could see his emotions.

This warehouse will make all the difference; it will open his way to more revenue, more profit. It promises to be the key to unlocking real success, yacht success, tell-the-world-to-fuck-off success.

The bottlenecks keeping him from fully maximizing sales had always been an impediment to growth, but no longer. He'd needed space to hold incoming supply, organize and sort it for his different customers, then efficiently move the product out and deliver it. Here it is, in this huge warehouse on the river in Pascagoula, Miss. A warehouse that had been empty and unused for who knows how many years.

It wasn't easy finding such a suitable location, but when he learned a customer of his security services company had some buildings laying fallow, he knew opportunity was hitting him upside the head like a two-by-four.

He crossed his arms over his barrel chest, his huge biceps bulging— a threatening appearance and in contrast to his face which, despite the scars on his left cheek and chin, looked almost childlike and giddy at that moment. Like a kid in a candy store for the first time, imagining the unlimited sweets to be plucked and savored soon.

A shadow appeared in the periphery of his vision. Someone was trying to get his attention.

He turned and saw Chad Broussard, a gangly twenty-something-year-old from Virginia that Mironoff thought of as his top lieutenant. Broussard's primary job was checking the incoming product, sorting it to match each customers' request.

It was an important job, and Broussard did his job well, seldom pestering Mironoff with unnecessary problems.

Mironoff slowly turned his head towards Broussard. Judging by the expression on Broussard's face, this must be a big problem.

"We got this new girl," Broussard said. "She's trouble."

"Trouble? How trouble?" Mironoff said in his jumble of dialects and accents, the result of a childhood in Eastern Europe, Venezuela, and other places he never revealed.

"She got a phone. Called someone."

Mironoff's face reddened. The cold in his eyes turned from November storm to permafrost. Broussard took a deep breath and prepared himself for what was next.

2

Montana Stone, "Tana" to anyone who knew her, looked at the Pinterest page on her iPad. The room was remarkably similar to her own living room: the room shown on her iPad had a similar wall of windows and seemed to be about the same size as her own.

She thought she liked the way the room looked, a cozy, over-stuffed sofa looking out on garden flowers and a green lawn through gauzy curtains. The room was bright and airy, making Tana imagine afternoons spent with hot tea and a favorite book in her hands. A chair for reading at one end of the sofa, perfect for Tension Tamer tea and maybe a P.D. James book or something by Grafton, with an end table and lamp next to it.

The chair on Pinterest was white, and Tana had found a chair nearly identical at the furniture store in Pensacola. A sofa similar to the one in the photo was more difficult, but she'd found an acceptable compromise at a store in Mobile.

She studied the room. As near a carbon copy of the Pinterest design as possible.

But having now assembled her living room using the new furniture and new curtains, something wasn't right. She studied the sofa, then the chair. Then the curtains, the matching set ordered from the supplier cited on Pinterest.

Something about it felt wrong. Made her feel wrong.

She slowly walked to the curtains and wrapped her fingers around the fabric, rubbing the silky surface. She closed her eyes. Thoughts of ripping the curtain down filled her mind, followed by the satisfied feeling of watching bits of threads in the air as the fabric is shredded. She envisioned little motes of polyester softly gliding in the living room air, swirling around her as she moved.

In her mind's eye, the little bits of fabric sparked into flames. Tana imagined the little flames combining, growing into larger and larger little fires, eventually igniting the curtains, the chair, the sofa. They combined into a blaze that grew, consuming the front window, then the house, then Tana herself.

She opened her eyes and released her clenching grasp on the curtain. She took in a deep breath and exhaled. Two more times…that's what they'd said to do when feeling stressed or overcome by emotion, right? Three deep breaths.

After exhaling the third deep breath, she grabbed the curtain again and yanked on it, pulling hard. She tore the curtain from the wooden rod extending across the windows, letting it fall in a heap on the floor.

She calmly stepped to the other curtain and ripped it down, too.

After stuffing the ruined curtains in a garbage bag, she threw in a pillow from the sofa. She also snatched a small, wooden carved dog from the end table that looked so sweet in the Pinterest page, and violently threw it in the bag.

"Can't take this," she said quietly while she stalked the room for more victims to add to the garbage bags.

She continued restlessly picking up and dropping things into the garbage bag. She stepped through her front door with the filled bag, her eyes tired and unfocused. She walked to the garbage can at the side of her house. She stood by her garbage can for several minutes before lifting the bag and dropping it in.

"Can't take having this around me."

She drifted back into the house and walked to her kitchen, then walked back into the living room. Then she went back to the kitchen and returned to the living room—two more times.

The third time she returned, her eyes took in the room as if for the first time. "Better," she said, looking about, trying to convince herself.

She picked up her iPad and looked again at the Pinterest page. Such a wonderful room, so well put together.

Tana stood behind her new sofa and ran her hands across the back, staring out the windows spanning the front of the room. The fabric was textured, thick threads that rubbed back against her fingertips. It was nice and relaxing to just stand here and feel the fabric.

Her mind shot back to a memory of doing the same thing in her parents' home in Missouri. Images of the dull plaid fabric of her mother's new sofa that was bristly and rough. Tana was stroking the sofa while tears rolled down her cheeks.

"We're not going to let that happen, Graciela," her father was telling her mother. He stood over Tana's mother as if she was a child herself, barely over five feet tall like Tana was now. Her long dark hair covered her face, and cascaded over her father's thick forearm. Tana remembered one of her mom's caramel-colored arms slinking around her father, gripping as tightly as she could.

And Tana was crying, but she didn't know why.

She shook herself out of the moment and looked down again at the sofa. *It's not mom's sofa, it's new and soft and mine*, she reminded herself. She suddenly began pacing about the room, her pent-up energy needing a release.

She sat in the sofa, then got up and went to the chair. Then returned to the sofa.

She was eight months from her job as a crime analyst in the St. Louis Metropolitan Police Department, ten months from the day she saw the body of her father, John Stone, on the floor in front of the plaid sofa.

She stood and paced again.

Her new life on the Gulf Coast wasn't helping her move past that day as well as she'd hoped.

She collapsed into a wooden dining chair at the reclaimed table that served as her desk. It was a small, rectangular dining table someone had tried to send to the garbage dump but Tana snatched it from the curbside. She ran her hand across the pitted surface of the table, feeling the edges of areas where chunks of finish had come off. She used the nail of her index finger to pick at the edge of the finish, and scratched at it until a flake peeled away from the wood.

She continued to pick at the table, focusing on her breathing and trying to avoid falling into another of the storms raging inside her, what she'd come to call her "head-icanes." The storms that took over and blocked all of her other thoughts, storms that swirled in her head and left her often feeling lost and confused.

Sometimes, the storms helped her find connections and patterns.

Why had the curtains made her so angry? She knew she wasn't a "girly-girl," that's for damn sure. She always told herself she'd never be that kind of woman.

But she seemed to like clutter and sweat and just a bit of dirt.

She picked off another chunk of finish from the table top. The flake popped off the wood underneath, then hit a thick folder near the corner of her desk. The folder had a big Stockton County Sheriff's Office logo printed on the front, with the words "Case File" below it. Inside were reports of a series of armed robberies that had occurred along the interstate highway in the northern part of the county. Investigators had been working on them for months, making little or no headway towards solving them.

That's when White Sands Chief of Police Jett Jeanrette suggested they contact Tana.

He assured them that Tana's experience in St. Louis could be helpful. He also reminded the county folks that it was Tana who stopped a serial killer named Joey Beaumont in White Sands.

But Jeanrette didn't ask Tana before he did. He just assumed since she'd been able to help stop a killer, that she'd be able to tie up these robberies.

Sure, no problem. Let's go pick at that scab. Thanks, Chief Jackass.

He did that two weeks after he'd last spoken to her. After he'd tried to confine her, tried to manipulate their budding relationship. Two weeks after she'd told him to go to hell.

Tana had applied her 20-years experience as a crime analyst in Police Intelligence in St. Louis to find the serial killer, but it cost her: she was almost killed and her only real friend was nearly murdered— and Jett only listened to Tana when the killer lashed out at her.

This is more bullshit I don't need, Tana told herself.

Besides, she came to White Sands to get away from police work, to stop being the weird woman who used her confused and obsessive thinking disorder to figure out what bad people were doing.

She stared at the Sheriff's Office logo on the folder. A gold, five-pointed star against an American flag. Her eyes traveled from point to point around the star, then locked onto the center of the star where "Sheriff's Office" was emblazoned, breaking down the design elements and analyzing the color choices (red for strength; blue for fidelity…but why gold? Why always gold?).

She shoved the folder into a corner of her desk. Again, three deep breaths to slow her heart rate.

Robberies were her specialty in St. Louis. Or rather, where her specialty until two robbers broke into her father's home and murdered him. Two robbers whose trail of violence she'd missed when analyzing a series of break-ins in neighborhoods near her father's house.

There was always a challenge in getting into the mindset of criminals—the easiest were addicts in need of money for drugs; harder were the desperate ones just needing quick cash. The worst did it for thrills and were even more difficult to analyze and anticipate.

Another deep breath. And again.

Each time she thought about the file and the big logo on it, she felt a shortness of breath.

She reached out and pulled the folder back out, staring again at the cover.

Finally, she flipped it open and began reading. She read through the reports, twice, and studied the notes made by investigators.

She read it all a third time.

There was something wrong about the way these robberies were going down—the pieces weren't fitting in her mind, no matter how she tried to push them together to make some kind of narrative. She wasn't seeing the solution.

Tana pulled open a drawer and grabbed a sheet of paper and a pencil. She returned to the front of the folder and began reading a fourth time, her hand scribbling words as she read.

Two men...guns...ski mask...no money taken...balaclava...food aisle...

After the fourth time through the reports, Tana dropped the pencil and suddenly pushed herself away from the desk.

She stood, closed her eyes, and did more deep breathing.

She tossed her notes inside the folder and slapped the cover closed. She needed new window coverings, not another case.

3

Black has shades. Or, at least, the black of night on the Gulf Coast does.

Robert Gulliford, a three-year veteran of the White Sands, Alabama, Police Department noted this as he cruised along Intracoastal Boulevard. Warm September air was blowing in through the open windows of his patrol car, fueling his wandering mind.

The road was all but empty, giving him the chance to consider the three levels of black ahead of him: the macadam black of the road below darker onyx sky, with dark ebony shadows of trees in the distance.

Katydids and crickets chirps filled the air. They were the only sounds heard at 4 a.m., except for the smooth, low rumble of the Dodge Charger Pursuit Robert drove.

He cruised at a leisurely pace, passing quiet neighborhoods and vacant lots to his right; to his left, a tall embankment that separated the roadway and much of the town of White Sands from the Gulf Intracoastal Waterway, a wide canal built to enable ships to pass from Mobile Bay to Perdido Key, in Florida, and eventually all across Florida without having to enter Gulf waters.

He slowed and pulled into a small strip mall. The Charger rolled through the parking lot as Robert used a spotlight to inspect the businesses for any signs of break-ins or bums. He used the spotlight's handgrip to maneuver the beam across the store fronts, momentarily illuminating them. There was a used clothing store featuring last year's shorts and tops—"Good as New! $5"; a barber shop with a dated political sign in the window that confirmed Robert's suspicion the place catered to men who were one, if not two, generations older than he; the red-and-gold trim of the Jade Dragon Chinese restaurant where he once watched a cockroach wrestle half a green bean across the floor; and an insurance agent's office devoid of any personality.

Nothing was amiss. Nothing is ever amiss.

Robert had come to understand the ebb and flow of night-time shifts in White Sands. After Labor Day was a quieter time of the year in the resort community, falling between the heavy summer season and the arrival of winter's "snow birds." In September and October, if there isn't a party to break up or a crash on a highway by 1 a.m., you're in for a long, quiet night. The seven-member police department is seldom tested on these nights. Often the biggest challenge is avoiding carelessness…or napping.

But still, you still never know what's around the next corner.

Satisfied in the security of the Towering Palm Shopping Center, Robert pulled back onto Intracoastal Boulevard and headed towards the next place to check, White Sands Masonry Supply, about a mile and a half further up the road.

Shortly after turning back onto the road, Robert noticed a small picnic area atop the canal embankment. The table was more inviting than the drive to the masonry supply, so he crossed over the median and pulled to a stop on the northside of the road. He picked up the police radio microphone and pressed the button to initiate contact.

"Dispatch, this is Unit 251," he said. "Reporting 10-10."

Static filled the radio's speaker momentarily, then stopped.

"OK, Bobby, let me know when you're back on," the voice said.

"Roger that." Robert slipped the microphone back into its holder on the radio mounted under his dash and opened his door. Stepping out into the night, he stretched his back and took a deep breath. He turned and reached into the car to grab a thermos resting on the passenger seat. He straightened up, closed the car door, then climbed the embankment to the picnic table.

He sat on the top of the table, putting his feet up on the bench, and looked around. The table was about 20 feet above the roadway on the crest of the embankment. He could see any traffic coming from a mile away in either direction.

He could even see any shrimp boats or private yachts navigating on the Waterway. As he sat sipping coffee, the lights of a vessel on the Waterway approached from the west. The vessel likely came from Mobile Bay, and was heading to Perdido Bay.

He watched as the vessel approached, and studied it as it motored past him. Robert recognized it as a barge, though not one pushing any cargo boxes in front.

The 120-foot long boat was an accommodation barge, built like a large houseboat capable of carrying and housing a work crew. This barge carried a two-story building on its decks that made it almost look like a floating Motel 6, painted blue on the hull and white above decks. He could see lettering painted on the starboard bow, probably the name of the craft, but he couldn't make out what it said.

The craft's diesel engines ran quietly, but as Robert watched, the droning sound of the engines dropped a notch. Then, the sound of water churning from the propellers stopped.

The barge drifted ahead on the water. After gliding for a while, the barge pulled towards the north shore of the canal.

It reached land maybe a thousand feet up the canal, and came to stop.

Even that far away, Robert could hear voices of the crew across the water. That was followed by the sounds of something heavy being moved, metallic squeals and clanging noises cutting through the quiet night.

He took a sip of coffee and watched. Lights on the barge flicked off, except for a pair of red lights on the stern.

Robert was letting his mind wander and began thinking about how to finish a bathroom he'd been working on when the noises from the barge stopped. The night was suddenly very still.

Robert had lived in White Sands for most of his life, spent much of his school break days fishing or swimming in the canal not too far from where the picnic table was where he first spotted the barge. As a kid, he used to dream of climbing aboard one of the luxury yachts that occasionally came by, or even taking a ride on a barge, working his way all the way up the Eastern Seaboard.

But none of the bigger boats ever stopped here—and if they did, what could he do? Jump 20 feet to the deck? No likely...

As he watched the barge, vehicle headlights approached the barge from the other side of the canal. A convoy of two or three vehicles broke through a row of thick trees and underbrush, then stopped near the canal's edge.

Robert stood and walked to the canal, trying to get a better view. He could see one of the vehicles that drove down to the canal was larger, maybe a small bus or a van, while the others were SUVs or possibly pickup trucks. The vehicles' headlights all switched off as he watched, followed by doors opening and closing.

Then Robert heard talking—no, not talking. The voices were firmer, harder, more like orders or commands being given.

Another sound carried across the water, more voices, but higher pitched and lighter. Something that sounded like a short scream.

He snatched his Thermos off the picnic table and jogged to the waiting Charger. As he cranked the wheel to pull out onto the road, he radioed in that he was back on duty and heading to check out a barge on the canal.

"What's your location, Robert?" the dispatcher asked.

"I'm just past the three-mile marker on Intracoastal Road," Robert said. "There's an accommodation barge docked on the northside of the canal. It sounded like they were unloading something."

"Bobby, there's no dock there. They can't be unloading."

"I know, I know, but something is going on. I'll check it out and report back."

He reached a small parking area near where the barge had stopped, and pulled off the road again. He grabbed a large flashlight and dashed up the embankment. From the top, he could see he had overshot the barge's landing spot a little. He was now about a hundred feet ahead of the barge now sitting silently in the dark.

Robert started walking towards the barge on a pathway that followed the canal's edge. He wanted to find out why they'd stopped there, where there's no dock. Maybe get the boat's registration number and name from the forward side of the craft. But he'd have to get closer for his flashlight to be helpful. With that information, he'd be able to find out the owner, if any following up was needed.

As he walked towards the barge, Robert tried to remember if there was any sort of a landing spot in this section of the canal. He was confident that no docks existed on the other side of the canal, other than the Havenport Marina, about a mile and a half back towards Mobile Bay. Another dock, or more accurately a shipping port, was located at the big storage facility built by BODE, Inc., the oil drilling company owned by billionaire Sandy Basko. The BODE facility was a little closer, but still more than half a mile from where the barge stopped.

He was just under fifty feet from the barge. He lifted the flashlight with his finger ready to switch it on.

A sudden bright spotlight above the barge's wheelhouse switched on before he could, blinding him. He stopped and raised an arm to shield his eyes.

Suddenly, the barge's engines roared to life and the vessel began moving backwards, back towards Mobile Bay.

Robert tried to run to catch up, but he couldn't see the path because of the blinding light. He had to slow down on the uneven pathway. When he tried to jog, he stumbled and nearly fell on the path.

The barge was gaining speed now, easily pulling further and further away. Across the canal, the three vehicles he'd seen pull up when the barge stopped started up and sped away.

"Damn it!" He stopped and turned to run back to his car. As he stepped off the path to run down the hillside, he caught his left foot in a rut. He fell and rolled several times before springing up to his feet halfway down the hill. He tried to jog, but a shot of pain in his ankle made him stop. Hobbled by the injured ankle, he limped towards the car as quickly as he could.

When the Charger's engine roared to life, Robert hit the gas pedal and slammed the gearshift into drive, spinning rocks and loose sand behind him. The rush of torque to the rear wheels pushed the back of the car sideways. He cranked the wheel and let the over-powered rear wheels push the car around in a spin until it was facing the direction he'd just come.

He was heading back in the direction he'd come from earlier, hoping to pass by the barge and get to the top of Mobile Road bridge where he could see the boat from above as it passed on the canal. If he could make it in time.

But getting to the bridge meant having to negotiate a series of turns before the bridge, where Intracoastal Boulevard ends. He'd have to take a hard left turn on Old School Road, go three blocks, then make a right. Mobile Road would be another two blocks down, and after another right turn onto Mobile Road, go half a mile back up to the bridge.

Robert kept his foot on the gas pedal as the car approached 100 miles per hour. He snatched the radio microphone and was about to report what he'd seen, but then put the radio microphone down. What had he seen? A barge heading down the canal? He needed more details before reporting it. Sure, there were some trucks driving on the other side of the canal, but what did it all really mean? In hindsight, he couldn't be sure.

He saw trees lining the canal illuminated by the barge as the Charger zoomed passed it. He flew down the road and reached Old School Road, where he had to slam the Charger's brakes, made the hard turn, then punch the gas again to speed up for three blocks.

He flew through the quiet residential neighborhood, then took the first right at 40 miles an hour. He slowed for traffic on Mobile Road, but was soon swinging around the corner and zipping towards the top of the bridge.

At the crest of the bridge, high over the canal, the Charger skidded to a stop. Robert jumped out of the car, momentarily forgetting about his quickly-swelling ankle until another flash of pain hit when he put his weight on it. He gingerly limped as quickly as he could to the railing over the canal.

The front of the backward-traveling barge was just going under the bridge. Robert turned and began to head across the roadway to the other side of the bridge, but had to stop for oncoming traffic. As he stepped onto the south-bound lanes, he could hear the sound of the barge engines clearing the bridge. By the time he reached the rail on that side of the bridge, the barge had sunk into the dark black shadows. It was too far away to see anything identifying the craft's registration or name or port.

He slowly limped back to his car, then drove it to the end of the bridge where he pulled off the pavement and parked. He pulled a notepad from his shirt pocket and started writing notes of things that he'd want to remember later, things like where the barge stopped, the color, size and markings on the barge, the sound of something being moved when the barge stopped, the voices.

4

The eastern sky was noticeably lighter by the time Robert pulled into the department's parking lot. He parked the Charger and lurched his way across to the sidewalk, wincing every time he put weight on his left foot.

He carefully stepped into the department's front office, where two other officers and the desk sergeant, a lean, deeply tanned man the other officers called "Shooter," were laughing about the upcoming Alabama football game.

"I'm taking the spread," Patrick DiCicco said. DiCicco believed he could predict games from the grumblings in coffee shops and diners he heard when out on patrol, despite his abysmal record in office bets. "No way we're beating LSU by ten."

A round of boos arose from the others, but was cut short when Shooter noticed Robert limping his way through the door. He quickly made his way to Robert and put an arm around Robert's shoulders to help him.

"What's happened to you?" Shooter said. He helped Robert walk to one of the office desks.

"I tripped, twisted my ankle," Robert said, slumping into an office chair. "I was trying to catch up to the barge I saw on the canal."

"Barge on the canal?" DiCicco said. "Kinda small water for a barge, ain't it?"

"No, we used to get barges along here all the time," Shooter snapped at DiCicco before turning back to Robert. "Why were you chasing a barge?"

Robert relayed the full story, including how he fell as he was running to his car to try, and his race to catch up to the rapidly departing barge.

"Ain't no barges on the canal anymore," DiCicco mumbled. "I can't remember the last time I saw anything like that."

"Yeah, well, if you were on the boulevard this morning, you would have seen one," Robert shot back. He was lifting his leg to carefully slide his shoe off.

"I can check with Pensacola Coast Guard to see if any shippers reported coming this way," Shooter offered. He watched Robert peel down the sock and was expressionless as Robert's ankle, which looked like a red softball, was revealed. Robert tenderly felt the swelling, then pulled the sock back over his ankle.

He picked up his shoe and started to put it back on, but winced and put the shoe down.

"I'll take you to urgent care." Shooter stood over him, measuring the level of pain registering on Robert's face.

"OK. Thanks, Shooter," Robert said. He stood up, holding his shoe in one hand and grabbing Shooter's shoulder with the other. "I'll do the reports when I get back. I tell you, this was something weird."

"What do you mean?"

"When the barge stopped, there were these three vehicles came down from Airport Road, I guess. I heard some yelling and stuff and then..." He grimaced as he absent-mindedly put too much weight on his injured ankle standing between two desks. "I heard some women or girls, I think. Talking at first, but then it sounded like a scream or a yell."

Everyone looked at him.

"A scream?" Shooter sounded dubious.

"Yeah, well, I don't know. Sounded like a scream." Robert wasn't sure what he heard now, back in the office, and surrounded by the others. "Something weird, though."

"Could it have been an owl or some bird?" DiCicco asked.

"Maybe a wild dog?" Joseph Hancock, the third officer and the department's newest. His lack of experience and insecurity showed in the lack of confidence with which he offered his suggestion.

DiCicco glared at him. "Shut up, Hancock." He crumbled up a sheet of paper and threw it at Hancock, hitting him squarely on the forehead.

"No. It wasn't birds and it wasn't dogs," Robert said. "I'm telling you, it was something else...something...not right."

Shooter exchanged looks with DiCicco, who turned back to his desk.

Shooter grabbed hold of Robert again. "DiCicco, call over to Mobile

Bay, and see if they can find this barge before we lose it in the bay traffic."

He helped Robert navigate through the counter that extended across the front of the office, keeping the public on one side of the room, and working officers on the other.

"Hancock, I got a job for you. Are you up for it?"

Hancock jumped up. "Yeah, Shooter. What do you need?"

"I need you to go to the store and get some fresh rolls for us for when we get back."

Hancock's shoulders dropped. He stood glumly for a moment, then started packing things in his uniform pockets: a pen, his phone, his notepad that was blank but for the little animal figures he'd drawn in the corner of each page to make a short animated cartoon.

He took three quick steps and got ahead of Robert and Shooter so he could hold the door open as Robert limped through it.

"Hope that's nothing too serious, Bobby."

"Thanks," Robert said. He was through the door and focused on stepping off the sidewalk without putting too much weight on his left foot. Once safely on the parking lot pavement, he turned towards Shooter.

"What do you think? I think maybe it was some kind of illegal business going on," he said. "Why else would they meet up with someone in the middle of the night, middle of nowhere?"

Shooter opened the passenger door to a police SUV for Robert.

"Doubt it." Robert stepped into the vehicle and Shooter shut the door. He walked around to the driver's side and got in before continuing. "Let's not get ahead of ourselves, Bobby. Probably just stopped for some kind of repairs. Maybe the motor wasn't running right and they met up with some mechanics."

As Robert thought about this, Shooter turned around to back the vehicle up and then headed to the urgent care center on Mobile Road.

"But what about the sounds? I'm telling you, something was off about the whole thing."

Shooter drove in silence for several blocks.

"You know this one night, I was setting out by the lagoon on break from patrol, just sitting there and I heard this really loud scream coming from just over a dune behind me. I ran over towards it, then heard it again further away so I chased after the sound. I came running around this bend and fell in the sand. When I did, this big…bird took off. It made the sound I heard and thought was a scream."

Shooter turned towards Robert and added, "It was a loon, those birds like a goose. Never seen one—or heard one—before or since, but they sound like someone screaming.

"I didn't know anything about them, had to look it up. Then I talked to this guy used to walk the beach every day who was into birds. He said it could definitely have been a loon."

He drove another few blocks.

"Guess it was, beings as we never found any body in the dunes…"

Robert was silent. He thought back about the sounds he heard and began to feel less confident of what he thought he'd seen and heard.

"I suppose. I don't know what I heard." He was looking out the window, watching the buildings and houses they passed.

Shooter filled the time telling Robert about some of the other calls the other officers had dealt with overnight, including a disorderly, and several people in a new development near the town's airport complaining about a loud plane landing and taking off after midnight.

"Overall, a pretty quiet night," he said. "I kinda like the quiet in these off-season months."

"Yeah, me, too," Robert said. "Reminds me of the way it used to be in town, before all them condos were built along the shore."

Both men knew what White Sands had been like before developers took advantage of cheap land and cheaper financing to buy up and build on the beach. For years, White Sands had lay fallow, drawing little interest from outsiders because of a series of catastrophic hurricanes in the 1970s that nearly wiped the town off the map.

But the memories of those storms eventually faded, and with a boom in vacationers heading to Florida, it wasn't long before town leaders in White Sands decided to become more friendly with well-financed developers.

Robert was in high school when builders completed a row of condo towers that lined the beach from the east end of White Sands to the middle of the growing town. Before then, local kids enjoyed miles of open beach, where they could play and swim most of the year on the beaches that gave the town its name. They were lords of the waves and dunes, spending sunny afternoons after school running up and down the shoreline, fishing for redfish and snappers and kingfish. During breaks between school terms, they all but lived on the beach, gathering early in the mornings and not heading home until well after sundown.

But as he watched the expanding line of condominiums, he knew his life in White Sands would not be the same. After high school, he enlisted in the Army and when his stint was over, he almost didn't return.

He came back to care for his ailing mother and it wasn't long before ideas of moving away just dissolved. He reconciled himself to staying and living in White Sands. Before he knew it, he was dating someone, then married and buying a small house. And Robert was in search of a better, more stable job. He applied to the police department and found a place where the others appreciated his military service and training as an MP.

"You know, I was just thinking how different the town feels the last few years," Robert said, distantly.

"How do you mean?"

"Well, everyone used to just live in neighborhoods along Mobile Road. You knew practically everyone and everyone knew you," Shooter said, then stuck a cigarette in his mouth. "When they first built those towers and the tourists started coming here, you knew who lived here and who didn't. But then they started building north of the waterway, and on Lafitte Island and things really changed."

He stopped talking and looked out the window. They were passing a new shopping center and the entrance to the airport.

"They built up that airport for all the rich people buying up LaFitte Island places," he said. "Used to be you couldn't fly here in anything bigger than a Cessna. Now, you got Gulfstream jets and loud helicopters coming in."

"Yeah," Shooter said. "Have you seen that big cargo plane in there? That one owned by BODE? I saw it take off last week—that was pretty cool."

"No. What kind of plane is it?"

"I don't know. Seems like it's the size of a 737—that's probably the plane people were complaining about last night. I didn't know planes that big could fly out of here."

The sign for the urgent care center came up on the left, so Shooter slowed and pulled into a turning lane. After three cars passed in the other lane, he made the left and pulled into the center's lot.

They got back to the station 90 minutes later. Robert had a plastic boot around his foot enabling him to walk without further injuring his ankle, but still limped to a desk before sitting down.

"How you doing, Robert?" Gwen, the department's administrator, secretary, and office mom, said. Gwen was most mothering when someone in the department was injured, no matter how minor or insignificant the injury was. She once forced DiCicco to stand still for 10 minutes while she washed and treated a small cut from a piece of glass he'd picked up at a crash scene. Before she finished, she had covered the cut with antiseptic and a huge bandage. "Let me get you some Tylenol. And a coffee…"

"No, thanks, Gwen," Robert said, smiling at her. "They gave me something at the clinic and I'm heading out as soon as I write a report on last night. But I appreciate you offering."

"Well, you need something, you just ask."

"My wife's in Tennessee visiting family," Robert said. "Can you bring me some of your fried chicken later? Maybe with some sides?"

"Watch it, young man," Gwen said. Her years in the department had prepared her for the teasing officers sometimes gave her, and she could often give as good as she got. "That reminds me, I was just looking at your training log. It seems you might be due for a refresher course in traffic control over in Montgomery…"

Everyone in the office groaned at the thought of the dull courses. Shooter walked by Robert and gave him a punch on the shoulder.

"Yeah, Robert, you need to get yourself over to Montgomery for a week," he teased.

"Hey, you made me mess up my report." Robert gave Shooter an exaggerated stare and crumpled the shift report form he was writing on. He made a show of pulling a fresh copy out of a desk drawer and placing it on his desk. "I see how y'all are now. Man gets injured on patrol, it's nothing to you."

He put his head down and went back to work on the report.

5

Thursday's morning traffic at Pixie's Beignet Bistro was always a good indicator of the weekend's level of tourism, as well as proof of the small shop's ability to provide treats capable of overpowering the willpower of even the most health-conscious dieter. The lure of warm pillows of fried dough under a mountain of powdered sugar was just too much; residents and tourists lined up together to kick start their days with a blast of fat, sugar and strong chicory coffee.

Tana sat at a small corner table with a cup of coffee on the table before her that was now well below the preferred temperature. She wasn't exactly a fixture at Pixie's, but regular enough that anyone who'd been there more than three times would know to avoid the woman who sat in the shop with a dazed and distant look on her face. If spoken to, she wouldn't answer. Most felt it was best to just leave her alone.

Repeat visitors on this day may have noticed her near-black hair tied in back with unusual carelessness—even for Tana. She used a thin green ribbon to tie her hair and the ends of the ribbons draped down one shoulder, boldly clashing against her orange top. Some people waiting in line to order their morning fix watched her as she sat without moving, gazing into her coffee cup or out the window at God knows what; her dark eyes not focused on anything at all, as far as they could tell. They didn't know her attention was locked onto something inside her head.

Right now, her attention was locked onto the word "balaclavas."

Tana found the sounds of the busy shop to be immensely helpful when she needed to work, adding background white noise that smoothed over peaks and valleys in conversations. It fed her meandering thoughts and helped let bits and pieces of ideas fall into place, like keys to unlock a crime.

Sometimes, when she wanted to link several pieces of evidence or connections between incidents, the noise even seemed to accelerate and propel her. She could relax and block outside stimuli, letting all the random facts of a case whirl through her mind until they grew into chains, DNA strands tying together to complete the story of a crime.

And from that, she could see the chain of events, from start to finish. She could then figure out how the bad actors could be stopped, and sometimes, how past crimes could be solved.

Not like her conscious thoughts, when her mind seemed a jumble of ideas, like a murmuration of blackbirds seeking a place to land. Sooner or later, it lands on an idea like, "Why not make my living room look like this picture on Pinterest?"

Her current trance started on the fact all of the clerks in the robberies she was studying for the Sheriff's Office said the robbers wore "ski masks," except one. One witness said, "balaclavas."

Tana didn't know why this stood out to her, although a balaclava mask is pretty much the same as a ski mask. If you're going to run into a convenience store for a quick grab-and-go robbery and have half a brain, you want to cover your face. Most of the time, the robbers in Southern Alabama skipped that, though, like they wanted to get caught. Some wrapped a scarf around their lower faces, Jesse James-style. After all, who in Southern Alabama would have a ski mask handy?

She remembered from her years in St. Louis that there, it seemed almost everyone had a ski mask. They weren't hard to find and were very helpful when temperatures dipped below zero in December and January.

This made it hard for the masks to be helpful for identifying anyone, since ski masks were ubiquitous during winter months, and didn't vary a great deal in color or style.

So as she reviewed security camera recordings from the convenience stores near Interstate 10 and the accompanying police reports for the robberies, she found herself wondering about balaclavas.

That's where her mind was when Robert Gulliford hobbled through the door to Pixie's and joined the line waiting to order. He didn't notice Tana until he was just about to order his half-dozen beignets and happened to turn to look back at the door as an elderly couple pushing walkers with coffees in hand struggled to exit. He turned to help when they negotiated their way through the door, then he spotted her sitting in the corner.

After ordering, Robert stepped over to Tana's table.

"Hey, Tana," he said.

She shifted her gaze from her laptop to his face and blankly looked at him.

"Oh, hi, Bobby," she finally said, her voice flat and distracted. "How long have you been there?"

He grinned.

"Just a moment. Y'all working on something? I can leave you be. Just wanted to say hi."

"No, I'm sorry. Please, sit down." She moved to push her laptop aside and watched as Robert struggled to sit down and maneuver his ankle boot into the aisle. "What happened to you?"

"I tripped last night; sprained an ankle. Did I interrupt your work?"

She didn't answer and reached for her coffee. "What do you associate with the word 'balaclava?'"

"Balaclava? What brought that up?"

"I'm looking at some robberies for the Sheriff's Office, and on the security cameras, you can see two men come in wearing balaclavas. Most of the clerks said they were wearing masks, but one correctly called it right."

"That clerk must have been in the service," he said. "I picture military, special forces. Or maybe a specialized police squad, like SWAT or a task force."

"Yeah. Me, too." She almost drifted away again, but then refocused on Robert's presence.

"I was just...I was thinking about some gas station robberies they had up along I-10," she repeated.

She took a drink of coffee, grimacing at the lukewarm, bitter brew. Robert watched as she drifted away again, her mind working out questions about the robberies. After another pause, she looked up at him and added, "Deputy Rogers at the Sheriff's Office asked me to take a look, see if I could help them get some idea of how to catch the robbers."

"Right."

Robert met Tana when she was working on finding Joey Beaumont. It was Tana who recognized how Beaumont was hiding, and selecting victims. He knew she excelled at spotting trends and links in crimes, and her strange way of thinking about things that caused her to over-analyze details others overlooked.

"So you're just coming off shift?" She lifted her coffee to her lips.

"My shift ended about four hours ago, but between getting shackled at the clinic…," Robert lifted his injured ankle, "… and writing my incident report, I'm just now going home."

Her eyes were blank for a minute. Then, she quickly looked at her watch.

"I'm sorry. How did you say you injured your ankle?"

"I saw this barge, what they call an 'accommodation barge' on the Intracoastal Waterway that stopped. I was going to check it out when it started to back up and I tripped when I was going back to my car. Graceful, huh?"

Tana sat silently, looking at him blankly again.

"Why did the—what did you call it, 'accommodation barge?'— stop? What is an accommodation barge, anyway?"

"It sort of like a floating hotel. They use them to move crews around to oil rigs and big river construction jobs. I'd never seen one before up here."

"So tell me what happened. What did you find out?"

Robert took a big drink from his coffee. He opened his mouth to begin explaining when the woman behind the counter called to him that his beignets were ready. He jumped up to pick up the box filled with hot pastries, struggling through the crowded shop on his way back to the table, then slid back into his chair, breathing hard.

"I was sitting on a picnic table having a coffee about four this morning when this thing goes by me. It stops and goes to the north-side shore a couple hundred feet further on. Towards Perdido. Florida. I don't know why it stopped but I heard some sounds, like a bunch of people, so I went up to check it out."

"I see."

"I thought I heard someone scream."

"Scream?"

"Yeah, well, everyone seems to think it was a bird or something. A loon, you know? But it didn't sound right to me. I tried to get a look at the name or number of the barge, but when I got close to it, they turned on a spotlight. I couldn't see anything. It started back-pedaling real fast—that's when I tripped, running back to my cruiser."

Tana was silent for a moment.

"What did Jett say?"

"I don't know yet, but Shooter said he didn't think it was anything. Says the barge probably stopped for a repair or something."

Tana watched Robert's face as he said this, noting he didn't seem to believe that. He picked up a hot beignet and took a bite, white powder falling from his mouth onto the box. He looked up at her and held a hand out, offering her one of the sweets.

"No, thank you," she said. She could tell Robert was trying to convince himself that he didn't see or hear something amiss, but wasn't doing a good job of it. "So, loons, huh? I didn't know you have loons in Alabama."

"Me, neither. Never heard such a thing, but Shooter told me he tracked one once because he thought it was someone screaming in the dunes. Guess they pass here migrating."

"So, this barge. How big is an accommodation barge?"

"They can be really big, almost like a small cruise ship, although I suspect they're pretty plain inside, being just for workers. This one wasn't that big as far as accommodation barges go, maybe eighty or a hundred feet long. Two floors. Probably hold thirty or forty people."

He finished his beignet and closed the box with the other five he'd ordered.

"I best be getting," he said, slowly standing and stretching. "I have another shift tonight and gotta sleep sometime between now and then. I'll see you later, Tana. Take care now."

"You, too, Robert."

She watched him walk out the door, holding it open as three muscular men walked in. As soon as Robert turned and let go of the door, the men stopped. They huddled just inside the door. One man looked back at Robert walking to his truck.

Tana watched as they turned and left the shop, but her attention was already drifting away from the conversation with Robert. Something about the videos of the robberies.

She turned her attention back to her laptop and opened a video file from one robbery.

In the video, two men came in with their faces covered. Whether by ski masks or balaclavas, their faces were covered. After entering, one went to the counter with a gun drawn while the other disappeared from view for a few minutes before re-appearing. The clerk had reacted quickly, handing over money, and the robbers left as soon as the second man reappeared.

She opened another file and watched a similar series of events. Except in this video, the clerk didn't hand over any money. He seemed confused about what to do as the robber demanded cash from the till.

But even though he didn't hand any money over, as soon as the second robber reappeared, they left.

Never seen that before, Tana thought.

6

Robert returned to the station at 6 p.m. that evening to begin his night shift. He'd gotten better at moving around with the ankle boot on, but was still a bit clumsy—he caught the boot on the door frame as he walked in, and while it didn't hurt, it did make a loud sound that startled everyone, including Jett. Three other officers, and two men picking up a copy of an accident report, all stopped and looked up simultaneously.

Everyone went back to whatever they were doing right away, except Jett. His six-foot, five-inch frame towering over the counter seemed to get even taller when he raised an arm to signal Robert to follow him as he turned and began walking towards the rear door of the office. He stood waiting while Robert made his way across the room.

"Hey, Chief," Robert said as he neared Jett.

"Robert," Jett said, nodding. "Let's go to my office for a minute."

Jett turned and started down the hall to his office, leaving Robert to follow as quickly as he could. When Robert stepped into the office, Jett was already seated and moving papers around on his desk. When he finished moving the papers, he put his hands together on his desk and looked at Robert.

"Read your report," he said. "How bad is the ankle?"

"It's nothing, really; doesn't even bother me anymore. This dang boot, though…"

"Do you have a follow up at the clinic?"

"Tomorrow."

"OK, good. I'm giving you a 24-hour administrative suspension. Check in with the clinic tomorrow, then come see me."

"No, Chief, really, it's fine."

"No, Bobby, really. You're done for the day."

Robert opened his mouth to reply, but Jett held up a hand.

"You're no good on patrol, you can barely walk with that thing— hell, you could barely run without it, apparently..." He was chiding Robert now, and Robert had to chuckle.

"I knew it would come to this sooner or later. 'Bobby got two left feet,' 'Bobby runs like a toddler with a full diaper,'" Robert said, smiling. "Go ahead, let's get it over."

"No, really, Bobby. You got injured on patrol so you're suspended until released by the doctor. It's what we call 'the law.' You know about 'the law?'"

Jett turned his attention to some papers on his desk.

"Go home. Go feed your chickens."

"I don't have chickens."

There was a pause in the conversation. Jett leaned back in his chair and clasped his hands behind his head, appraising Robert.

"So what's up with this accommodation barge you say you saw last night?"

"I don't know. It must have pulled in for repairs. We got anybody in town that might be expert in fixing something like that? Seemed like some SUVs and a bus came to meet the barge."

Jett mulled this over. "No commercial mechanics here work on something that big, except maybe at BODE."

"That would make sense, I guess, since the barge stopped right by the access road that runs down from the BODE entrance." Robert waited a minute before adding, "But then, why not use the BODE dock back by the marina? Why stop someplace there's no dock or easy access? And what about the noises I heard?"

"Don't know, but it ain't against any law. Maybe there wasn't an available berth; maybe the mechanics weren't with BODE. Could be a lot of things, Bobby."

"I know, I know, but it just didn't sit well. I'm telling you, there was something weird going on. The sounds I heard weren't loons, like Shooter and them said."

"What sounds?"

"Sounded like women, like girls."

Jett sat up.

"Women, huh? On an accommodation barge? What are you thinking—they're part of the crew? Entertainment for rig workers?"

"I don't know, Chief. Could be, I guess."

"Bobby, we don't really have any reason you need to be here. You patrol that road all the time and never saw a barge like this on it. Sounds to me like a one-off, most likely an emergency repair stop. You can forget about this and when you're off suspension"—Robert noted Jett had to add this little reminder— "Come back with a clear head."

"All right. Do you have my shift covered? Need me to hang here in case anything comes up?"

"We have it covered and no, I don't want you here. See, that's sorta how 'suspension' works."

Jett made air quotes around "suspension."

They both stood and Jett watched as Robert made his way for the door. As he stepped into the hall, Robert turned his head and said, "I saw Tana at the beignet shop this morning. She's working for the Sheriff's Office on some burglaries."

"That's what I heard," Jett said, flatly. He glared at Robert momentarily, telling Robert he'd stepped over a line he didn't know existed. Talk around the office had been that Jett and Tana were, if not an "item," becoming good friends. But Robert didn't always catch the latest gossip and tended to mind his own business.

Apparently, he had missed a crucial update.

Jett followed Robert to the front door and held it open for him without saying more. He walked alongside Robert as they walked towards Robert's red Chevy Z-71 truck, all the while Robert making small talk about the upcoming Alabama football game. Jett only grunted as they walked.

Jett stood by while Robert climbed into the high seat of the truck.

"I'm no doctor but I'll bet they told you to keep your leg up and let it rest," Jett said. "You do that today, see them tomorrow, and I'll talk to you after that."

"Yes, sir," Robert said, giving Jett a military salute. He started up his truck and pulled out of the lot.

He drove up Mobile Road towards the turnoff to his home, but when he came up on Airport Road, he made a sudden right turn. He watched his mileage to approximate the location where the barge had stopped, slowing as he approached. He was at the intersection of Airport Road and BODE Drive, an access road paved to the entrance to the company's enormous facility for its oil drilling endeavors.

He looked down BODE Drive as his truck rolled into the intersection. This seemed to align with the spot where the barge stopped, so Robert turned and followed the road south towards the waterway. As he went by the entrance gate to BODE, Inc., a mile and a half down the road, he saw the shadowed outline of a guard's head inside the guard house watching him.

Further on, the pavement ended and BODE Drive turned into a dirt-topped road flanked by trees on each side.

Robert continued for another quarter-mile before the road ended at the waterway. He parked his truck and climbed down. He walked over to the water lapping gently at the sides of a ten-foot drop-off. A gap in the trees to his left revealed a clearing on the other side.

He turned and limped his way through the gap and into the open space.

The area was about forty feet in diameter, cleared of all weeds and brush, with a clay surface hard-packed enough to be a suitable for a tennis match. Robert hobbled around the perimeter of the clearing, hoping to see footprints or find something tossed on the ground that might satisfy his curiosity.

He walked nearly the entire circumference before coming to a small path leading down to the waterway's edge. The ground made a gentle drop to the water here, so instead of a ten-foot drop to the water, the water here was only about four feet below the edge.

Perfect for a landing, he thought.

Robert looked around and noticed a small piece of colorful fabric torn by a sticker on a small blackberry bush about a foot off of the path fluttering in the slight breeze. He carefully stepped over to the bush and pulled the cloth free. Holding it up, he could see it was a thin, soft fabric, with swirls of green, yellow, and red.

He slipped it into his pocket and started back towards the clearing. Just before stepping off the trail, he noticed footprints in the softer dirt next to the path.

He kneeled and inspected the prints. They were small and light impressions. Light, but very clear. And judging by the textures of the soles of the shoes, Robert counted no less than four different people who had walked alongside the trail.

He also estimated the heights of the people leaving the prints, based on the distance between the steps of matching prints. He figured people between 56 inches and 66 inches tall made the footprints.

Robert pulled the swatch of cloth out of this pocket. He held it up again and studied it, then looked down at the footprints. There was no mistaking it—a group of women or girls had been here and made the impressions.

He walked back to the clearing and started towards his truck. Just before reaching the trees, he noticed something he hadn't seen before: an eight-inch pole planted next to one of the trees. His eyes followed the pole to the top, where a security camera was mounted.

Robert followed the view of the clearing the camera must be able to capture, and it was apparent the camera could view the entire area, and most of the path leading to the waterway.

A small, blinking red LED light flashed on the camera.

Why would someone have a security camera mounted here? Why would they be watching the clearing and the path to the waterway? Robert looked around again. To his left, a wide, empty field gave extended to the north as far as the airport, two miles up.

He was convinced that whatever he'd seen last night was connected to the footprints and the torn piece of thin fabric he found. Time to talk to Jett again.

He climbed into his truck and turned around to go back to the station. He drove up BODE Drive towards Airport Road, passing the entrance to the BODE facility.

7

Mironoff looked at the thick Omega watch on his wrist. Thirty-five minutes. How long is this asshole going to go on?

He was confined in the conference room at BODE, Inc., listening to an "expert" in electronic surveillance that wanted some of Sandy Basko's money currently flowing into Mironoff's pockets. He clearly didn't know shit, Mironoff thought.

"I would recommend installing hi-resolution cameras at these locations," the man whose name Mironoff had forgotten said while pointing to several places on a map of the BODE facility. "That will provide the additional security you need to receive the contract from Exxon-Mobile."

Sandy Basko, his squat body filling a chair at the end of the table raised up to put him several inches taller than anyone else sitting at the table, looked at Mironoff. He raised an eyebrow, while Mironoff appeared to be picking something from his fingernail.

"Well?" Basko said. "What do you think?"

"I think it's great idea." Mironoff said. His rumbling voice flat.

"Well, thank you, Mr. Miro—"

"But it's completely unnecessary." Mironoff slowly pushed back from the table and stood.

He took two steps towards the man and towered over him, even as the man took three steps back. Mironoff radiated trouble the way the sun radiates heat.

Mironoff stopped in front of the map. He acted as if he was studying the map, waiting to hear impatience grow at the table behind him. He crossed his arms and tilted his head.

Finally, he turned to the expert.

"Five years ago, I put cameras here, here and here." He stabbed the map with one of his thick fingers at each location, without turning to the map. "I didn't put one here, because you obviously didn't notice the way the HVAC unit blocks the view of the doors from that spot. I put it where it would do some good."

He glared at the man.

"What was your name? I forgot already."

"Uh...Jason Ribard. Top Flight Security Engineering."

Ribard was standing in the corner of the room. He shifted his weight, beads of sweat forming on his upper lip.

"Ribard? Jason Ribard?" Mironoff said, twisting his face with a look of confusion. He looked at Basko. "Isn't Jason Ribard in movies? Isn't there an actor 'Jason Ribard?'"

"Robards, Jason Robards," Basko said. "What's your point?"

"No point, Mr. Basko. I was just confused for a moment because what this man says we should do, we did."

Ribard stepped forward. "I inspected all locations and there are no cameras at these spots. You've done a terrific job at identifying many of the weak spots, but I'm afraid, not all."

Mironoff's face turned red. He smiled like a tiger about to engulf its prey.

"Let me ask you, you are expert? You are familiar with DVC Bluelight Wi-Fi cameras?"

"I know of DVC's cameras, yes."

Mironoff took one step in Ribard's directions and was face-to-face with the man.

"I didn't ask you if you knew their cameras, did I?"

Ribard looked at Basko for help, but didn't find any.

"No, I don't know about their Blue—what did you call them, Blueline cameras."

Mironoff turned and went back to his chair, settling into it. He turned his attention to Basko.

"Mr. Basko, please. This man knows nothing. I don't know why he is here. We have installed security system second to none—CIA should be so lucky to have something like you have."

He looked at Ribard again.

"This is third time you've had me in to hear these people who don't know their own business."

He took a deep breath and sighed. "And here you already have a system years ahead of what they even know about."

"So, what are these Bluelight cameras?" Basko asked. He noticed Mironoff had slipped into his peculiar accent, letting articles and conjunctions slip away.

"Old. Outdated. Piece of shit. I replace them in July with better, newer designs."

Basko studied Mironoff's face. He didn't like the man, but when it came to security, Mironoff knew more than anyone else he'd ever known.

Plus, the man alone looked like a nightmare—anyone caught embezzling, stealing, or trying to remove documents would prefer a few simple years in prison to a five-minute interview with Atlas Mironoff.

Basko stood and turned to Ribard. "I want to thank you for coming in today, Mr. Ribard," he said, extending a hand. "Please give Jim my thanks for introducing us."

Ribard gathered his material and started for the door.

"Mr. Ribard," Mironoff called out. "Good luck on Academy Award."

He waved as Ribard slipped through the door quietly.

Basko glared at Mironoff.

"Atlas," he said, exasperated. "Was that necessary? Christ, I pay you enough. Can you learn how to deal with these things a bit better?"

Mironoff gave Basko a leering smile.

"I'm sorry. I'm only trying to guard you from these people trying to steal your money." He had turned his huge hands upward, like a supplicant at church pleading for grace. "I am thick in the head, in some ways…but I know how to protect you and your business."

Basko studied him for a minute, thinking of the best way to respond to Mironoff's statement.

"Then how come I got material disappearing, and my last three bids were undercut by them sons-a-bitches at Bakken Well Services?"

Mironoff glared at him. "Sometimes, the little owl sees more than big hawk."

Basko snorted and stood up. He started for the conference room door. Two other company executives were in the room and when they realized Basko was headed out, they scrambled to exit with him.

Mironoff's attention returned to his fingernail.

"Götümü yala," he cursed under his breath as Basko left the room.

A phone in his pants pocket buzzed, and Mironoff saw a man he employed for the BODE security room was calling.

"Better be important. Better be fucking life or death."

"I'm sorry, Mr. Mironoff. I thought you should see something from the landing site."

"I'll be right there."

Mironoff made his way to the small hut at the eastern edge of the complex housing the company's surveillance equipment and crews. He opened the door and stepped into the pitch-black room illuminated only by a bank of monitor screens mounted to the wall.

Most displayed static images of areas around the grounds of the BODE property, but one screen was static. The image showed a man frozen in the middle of a dirt clearing.

"This man was at the landing site a few minutes ago," one of Mironoff's employees wearing their trademark black polo shirt with a small symbol on the chest said. "I thought you should know."

"Why? Kids and guys fishing go there all the time. What makes this guy so special?"

"I think he's the cop from last night."

Moron stepped closer to the screen. "You think?"

"Yes. I mean, he is the cop." The guard pushed a button beneath the monitor next to the one Mironoff was studying. The image on the monitor changed to one showing a man on ground next to water, a man dressed in a White Sands Police Department uniform. "This is from the barge last night. Facial recognition matched it."

Mironoff looked from one monitor to the other, comparing the images.

"He went to the site and was looking around

"Yes."

The guard didn't know what that meant, so he simply stood still and waited.

"Do we know where this man is now?"

"Yes. Courant and Davis are following him on Mobile Road."

"OK. Let me know when he is someplace where I can meet him."

8

Traffic was steady, not as heavy as the summer months see but with the sunny, Autumn days keeping some tourists in town, still pretty thick. Robert rolled down a window and hung his arm out, catching air in his hand. A sudden movement in his rearview mirror caught his attention, and he looked to see what it was.

The cars and trucks behind him were all rolling along down Mobile Road at almost the same speed, keeping even distances between them like vehicles in a 50-mph parade.

He turned his attention back to the road ahead, and starting thinking again about the barge, and the clearing, and everything that had happened.

He tried to conjure up the sounds he heard last night, but struggled to recall them. He just remembered how he felt when he heard whatever it was he heard.

Then, there's the piece of cloth, and footprints around the clearing he was just at. Maybe it's just a coincidence, but Robert couldn't let it go.

Behind him, an SUV made a quick lane change, squeezing into a narrow gap between two cars. One driver angrily honked, but the SUV pressed ahead, making another quick lane change.

Robert looked back at the honking, catching a glimpse of the SUV sliding in aggressively behind a family in an older pickup cruising in the other lane just a little behind Robert.

Another car honk again drew Robert's attention, and he looked in his mirror again. This time catching a view of the SUV pulling behind the car just behind him.

The big SUV had darkly tinted windows, and Robert recalled seeing a similar vehicle pulling out from BODE earlier. Is it the same vehicle?

But why would it be? The company seemed sure to have lots of vehicles for employees' use, and in the hot Alabama sun, tinted windows aren't unusual.

It seemed so cliche to drive a big, black SUV with tinted windows, Robert thought. What were they, super-spies heading to a pickup at the drive-through window at Mickie D's? You really couldn't drive a more obvious vehicle than a tinted-up, black SUV like it's *Mission Impossible*. He took another quick look in his mirror. The car between the SUV and his truck had turned off, and the SUV was accelerating towards Robert's bumper.

Robert decided to put some distance between himself and the obnoxious, dark vehicle. He switched lanes and sped up Mobile Road.

The SUV stayed with him, mirroring each move he made.

He intentionally slowed and sped up a couple of times, watching the response by the SUV's driver each time he did, and soon, there was no doubt the driver was very skillfully maintaining a fixed distance.

When traffic stopped at a light at the intersection with a county road that led to the big outlet center, the SUV rolled up behind him. Even with the vehicle so close behind him, Robert still couldn't see the driver or occupants inside it.

To see how far the driver in the ominous vehicle was willing to go, Robert decided to force his way into the flow of traffic crossing on the county road. He jammed on his gas pedal as a break in the traffic just big enough for him to pull into came through, and quickly merged with the eastbound traffic.

As he fell in line with the cars in the next lane, he watched for any signs of the SUV. If he saw it again, it would be clear they were following him. But if the SUV's driver wanted to catch up, he'd have to drive more aggressively, dangerously even, and shift between lanes to get through the cars behind Robert.

He looked in his rear-view mirror—the SUV was just barreling around a car only a few hundred feet behind.

There was no doubt in Robert's mind someone sent the vehicle after him, and it seemed likely it was BODE.

Had he seen or heard something they didn't want known?

How strange to be the one hunted, Robert thought. In Afghanistan, he was the hunter, the one doing the chasing. He remembered a dark night, lost in Kabul after chasing a carload of partying Coast Guardsmen enjoying a weekend getaway from their deployment to

Kandahar Airfield, where they performed inspections of shipping containers ferrying equipment and supplies to the airfield.

The Guardsmen had hooked up with Kashif, a local character known for leading U.S. soldiers to the city's more nefarious nightclubs. Nightclubs where the soldiers were often relieved of their wallets, watches, and sometimes, a few teeth.

He had followed the Guardsmen through the heart of the city, but then lost sight of them in a confusion of a neighborhood, one with streets that curled around nondescript, stone structures like a wide, dirt vine. He tried to double back, but got lost in the tangle of streets and turns and dead-ends.

Neighborhoods like that don't exist in White Sands, where lots and roads were plotted with a ruler's straight edge. The closest thing to Kabul's meandering roads and intertwined neighborhoods is the circular lanes of the Flamingo Outlet Mall, a mecca for tourists, just ahead on the left. The center featured two concentric circular rings of stores, with parking between the rings of stores and a small grassy park-like area at the center.

Robert changed lanes, then made a quick turn into the shopping center's parking lot. Robert drove to a lane between the buildings and followed it almost all the way around before parking his truck.

He slid out of his truck and walked as fast as his ankle boot would allow to a nearby GAP store.

Once inside, he stepped around a window display where he could appear to be shopping while also keeping an eye on the parking area.

He picked up a shirt as if to inspect it. As he put the shirt down, the SUV pulled into a parking spot near his truck. Robert watched the SUV for a few minutes. No one got out; the vehicle was like a dark cloud resting on the parking lot.

He felt unsure of what to do next. A call for back-up seemed like a good idea, but when he patted his pockets for his cell phone, he realized he'd left his phone plugged in and charging on the console in his truck.

As Robert kept one eye on the SUV in front of the store, he checked around the store, noting where exits were, where open spots could he could make a stand if needed, and where he could get trapped by a few men.

In seconds, he had worked out several plans and responses to an attack. He was ready.

The SUV started up and slowly backed out. It turned and drove out of sight, making Robert's response planning moot.

He relaxed and started to walk around the store. He dawdled, flipping through a rack of shirts offered at closeout prices. He pulled out a brightly colored sport shirt he liked, so he took it to the cashier and bought it.

Walking to his truck carrying the shirt in a small bag, Robert found himself still scanning the parking lot for the SUV. He didn't know what the driver or anyone inside the SUV might look like, but figured they would stand out among the aimless tourists strolling through the stores. He watched for people moving with a mission and saw none.

When he got back to his truck, he circled the parking lot twice to look for the black SUV before heading out.

There was no sign of it.

Finally, Robert exited the shopping center and drove to Mobile Road. He turned onto the southbound lanes to drive back to Sunset Road, the two-lane road that went west, towards Mobile Bay and his little farm.

Robert always rushed home after his shifts. He loved his shady little piece of Alabama, and loved sharing it with his wife, Alicia, and Tommy, the couple's three-year-old son.

But Alicia and Tommy were in Tennessee visiting Alicia's parents, and he'd only be greeted by an empty house. So he drove slowly, enjoying the afternoon and focused his thoughts on the bathroom project. He wanted to get it done before Alicia came home in three days, and he worried the ankle boot would slow his work.

He reached his driveway and pulled into the property, passing a stand of trees and bushes that shielded the house from the road, and let his truck roll to a stop alongside the house.

He pushed the truck's door open, then turned to grab his shopping bag when he sensed movement just outside the open truck door.

As he turned to see what it was, a large man stepped in front of him. The man held up a small, square box, and before Robert could react, the box made a blue flash.

Robert felt two painful jolts in his chest. His body convulsed, and he grunted in pain before sliding out of the truck. When he hit the driveway, his body continued jerking spasmodically for a moment before becoming still.

Robert lay in a twisted heap, unconscious.

Three men gathered and stood over him.

"Pick him up and put in him in the back," a short, thickly built man with a low forehead and heavy eyebrows said. "Better bind his arms and legs, too."

9

Despite a clear blue sky and bright sun, the Gulf surf was heavy and pounded on the beach in thunderous waves when Tana went for her morning run.

She ran along the waterline taking long strides that put her at a near sprint. She had learned to run near the water, where the sand was hard packed by the waves coming off the Gulf, since moving to White Sands six months ago, and was now a regular among the locals—who made sure to step out of her way on the beach.

Most of the others on the beach were familiar to her now, but she still studied each face she saw. In a second, she took in their eyes, whether shifty or steady, and their hands (did they hold or clutch?). Even the way they walked.

The gazebo at the public beach loomed ahead at the top of a dune and she turned towards it. She sped past the shaded benches and the parking lot, then continued her run to Mobile Road and the last mile of her morning routine.

Once home, she checked her phone. Jett had texted while she was running, but she hadn't read it. Whatever he wants can wait.

She grabbed a bottle of water and lifted to drink when her phone rang. Jett, again.

"Hello, Jett." She kept her voice flat, wanting to sound strictly professional.

"Tana, I'm sorry to bother you, but I need your help."

Sure, more help. Why not?

"What's up?"

"Robert is missing."

It took a minute for her to register what Jett said. She just saw Robert at the coffee shop two days ago.

"What does that mean?"

"Alicia, that's his wife, called me about five o'clock this morning and said she hadn't been able to get ahold of him in the last two days," Jett said. "I gave him a one-day suspension because of his ankle Thursday. I didn't hear from him yesterday."

You should have followed up when he didn't show yesterday, Tana thought. She tried to remember if Robert had said anything about going away when she saw him, but he didn't say anything about leaving town or going out on the Gulf.

"I went to his house and his truck was there, but he isn't," Jett continued.

"Where are you now?"

"I'm on Mobile Road, on my way back to his house. We took a quick look this morning, but we're going to give the area a more thorough look."

Jett took a deep breath.

"Tana, look, I didn't want to bother you. I know I pushed you too hard on the Beaumont case, and I know I kinda crowded you after... I'm sorry, it's just..."

Silence lingered as he drifted off.

"Tana, I just...well, I..."

"I get it, Jett. Don't get yourself tied up about it."

More silence.

"Well, I'm sorry, Tana. But right now, I really do need you." He paused and played his ace card. "Robert needs you. I don't know what's going on and I'm frankly scared."

Jett gave her the address of Robert's farm and she said she'd be there as soon as she could. Minutes later, she jumped into her Jeep and headed to Robert's place.

At the farm, she pulled in behind a line of police vehicles parked in the driveway. She spotted Robert's truck, parked in front of the cottage-style house encircled by a wide porch. The house was immaculately white, with black shutters on the windows, and for a moment, Tana feared she was looking at a Pinterest page again.

As she got out of her Jeep, she heard a woman shouting and turned to see a tall, blonde woman in her 20s yelling at Jett as he tried to hold her shoulders.

Alicia.

What do you tell a young woman when her husband vanishes? If it was someone other than Robert, you could say he's probably out with some buddies, fishing on the Gulf or camped somewhere on Mobile Bay. Or maybe you could say that he might be out with some people, maybe even another woman. But you knew that he'd be back, he always came back.

But you couldn't say that now because Robert wouldn't fail to let Alicia know if he was going fishing or stopping by to buy a part for his truck or some project on his house. He just wasn't the kind of guy to go hang out with drinking buddies or other women. If Robert wasn't on the job, he was with Alicia and the baby. He had turned down every invitation to after-shift gatherings, every offer of meals. He hardly even ever stopped at a store on the way home, he was always so eager to be with his family. For Robert, the route home after every shift was a straight beeline.

Tana slowly walked towards Jett and Alicia, then spotted Shooter across the yard with a group of officers looking around at the ground. She turned to check with him instead, before having to deal with Jett. As she drew near, she saw they were studying the dirt driveway that encircled a palmetto in front of Robert and Alicia's house before returning to the main driveway.

She gave the bare ground a wide berth as she approached.

Shooter looked up. "Hey, Tana, how y'all doing?" He spoke quietly, but she still sensed his fear and worry.

"I'm fine, Shooter. How's it going? Gotten any ideas on what's happened?"

Shooter took a deep breath and punched out one word, "No."

She studied the other officers as they followed tire tracks in the dirt. Shooter followed her eyes, then took a step towards the others.

"We spotted some tracks here that don't match tires on Robert's truck. They pull off the driveway kinda going in the wrong direction." He pointed to the spot where the dirt road rejoined the paved driveway. "Alicia's been visiting her folks up north for the last week and since it rained here day before Robert's last shift, we're looking at this as probably related."

Tana knew the weather in White Sands can help pin down events—the sandy soil didn't hold tracks well in rain but made a nice mould when damp. Sand packs tightly into the treads of shoes or tires and hold its shape until squashed or rain falls, erasing it like a kid's Etch-a-Sketch.

"So no one's been with him or talked to him since yesterday?"

"Far as I know, Jett's the last to talk to him," Shooter said. "Sent him home 'cause he sprained his ankle chasing a barge on the Waterway on patrol that morning."

"I saw him after his shift. He told me about the barge."

"What time did you see him?"

"I guess about 10:30…maybe a little earlier." She tried to remember what time it was when she saw Robert, but she was at the shop for three hours and for most of that time she was completely unaware of what happened around her.

A door slammed behind her, causing her to jump. She turned to see Jett walking quickly in her direction. His face contorted in anger, frustration and concern.

When he got close enough, Shooter nodded his head in the direction of the house and said, "She giving it to you good."

"Yeah, well, I can't say I blame her," Jett said. "I tried to calm her down. I just don't have any ideas of what could be going on."

He looked at her, studying her face and the way her eyes looked up at him.

"Tana, thanks for coming. And any help you can give us."

"No problem." She turned to continue studying the driveway, breaking away from Jett.

Jett then called out to the other officers, rounding up a crew made up from police and Sheriff's Deputies from across the south end of the county. When they circled around him, he directed them to various parts of the yard and told them to go search in those areas.

"I don't care if it's an old candy wrapper, a cigarette butt from 1975, or a dead squirrel. You find anything out there, bring back here. Let Shooter or me know what you got."

The officers fanned out across the long property surrounding the house. It was tidy and carefully organized. Three rows of pecan trees extended back from the house, shading the entire farm.

Tana envisioned Robert out tending to the thin grass in front, picking up branches that had fallen from the trees in back.

"Tana, Shooter—come with me. We can take a look inside."

The three of them walked to the front porch, climbing the five steps that ended at the front door. Jett pulled open a storm door, knocked on the inside door and pushed it open.

Alicia sat in a sofa to the left of the doorway, her eyes red and hard. She was tense, sitting with one knee raised with a foot on the edge of the sofa, with her arms clenching around them. One hand held a cellphone which was taking a beating from her thumb frantically typing out text messages.

"'Licia, we're just going to see if we can find anything helpful inside, like I told you," Jett said in his most reassuring voice. Tana remembered that tone. "I promise we won't be but a minute."

Alicia glared at the three of them for several seconds, then went back to her phone without saying a word.

Tana studied Alicia's determined face. She remembered someone—was it Robert?—telling her Alicia had also been in the service, but she'd forgotten which branch. Alicia was focusing her energy on following up with any of the local businesses Robert did business with, texting to Mose Richards, the mechanic Robert liked to have work on his truck, and Mason Johns, a onetime contractor who lost his business after the housing crash in 2007 and now made a living doing handyman jobs around the area.

She had already called hardware, paint, and farm stores Robert frequented; none recalled him stopping by in the last day or two, but two promised to check their records and to let her know what they found.

She turned her attention to the room. It was nicely decorated with furniture that looked at least a few years old but still in good shape—not Pinterest-ish, she noted, but still nice. Maybe she should take a photo to study later, she thought.

A line of pictures lining one wall showed Robert and Alicia on their wedding day, Robert in his Army fatigues, and Alicia in a Navy officer's dress uniform sporting the double bars of a lieutenant. Another grouping of photos captured the couple with their newborn son and several pictures of him as a toddler.

There wasn't anything that appeared moved or disturbed in any way as far as Tana could tell— apparently as far as Jett or Shooter could tell, either, as they had already stepped into the hallway that led to the bedrooms. She caught up to Jett and Shooter, who were studying a bathroom off the hallway.

When she looked inside, she saw what had caught their attention. The bathroom had been completely dismantled, the sink and vanity gone, the toilet removed and the walls from the front to the back around the tub bare to the two-by-four studs.

Jett and Shooter were discussing Robert's plans to redo the bathroom and surprise Alicia when she returned from Tennessee. Tana stepped past them, and continued down the hall, peeking into the room Robert's son slept in, and a spare room used as an office and guest bedroom.

At the end, the hallway went straight into the master bedroom. Tana stepped in and looked around. The luxurious touches in the room impressed her, touches that didn't match the rest of the house—maybe Robert had already fixed up the room. If so, to her eyes, he did damn good work.

She turned around and went back down the hall, then turned right to the kitchen. Jett and Shooter were already in the kitchen, looking around again for any signs of disturbance. Tana did the same. Again, nothing out of place.

"All right, let's go," Jett said and led the way to the door. He held the door open for Shooter and Tana, then said he'd be right out. He turned back to talk to Alicia.

Outside, Tana and Shooter went down the steps and walked to Robert's truck. She inspected the truck, stepping closer to the driver's side door to look in.

As she leaned closer to the truck, she felt the door give a little. She stepped back and could see the door was open slightly.

"Shooter, did you look inside the truck?"

"Not yet."

"The door isn't closed all the way. Do you think that means anything?"

Shooter studied the door.

"Could be. Let me get some gloves."

Jett walked out of the house and came over to the truck.

"You OK?" Tana asked him.

"No." His face had a hang-dog look about it that she hadn't seen before—even when he was struggling to solve murders, Jett maintained a steadfast grip on his emotions. This was new.

He turned to look at the officers searching around the yard, two of them nearly a hundred feet away at the back of the property. "I just can't figure what might have happened to Robert."

She felt a touch of sympathy for Jett. Or maybe it was a touch of joy after having watched another woman berate him so harshly.

Shooter snapped latex gloves over his hands, pulling her out of her thoughts. She watched as he carefully examined the door, then reached up to the top corner of the door frame. He pulled the door and it swung open—it wasn't even latched.

Shooter stepped around to the outside of the door and began to sprinkle the fine powder used to capture any fingerprints or marks on the truck. Jett studied the inside of the vehicle.

Robert's phone was on the floor and a bag from the GAP store rested on the center console. Jett lifted the bag and pulled out the shirt Robert purchased. The store receipt fell out of the bag and dropped to the floor of the truck.

He reached in and picked up the receipt, reading the timestamp of the transaction: 7:45 p.m. He handed it to Tana.

"That's about an hour after he left my office," Jett said.

"He goes from the station to the store; goes home, then…what?" she said. She looked around, hoping to see something helpful, something out of place…just something. "Leaves the door of his truck open and his phone and a new shirt in the truck…"

Shooter stepped around the door.

"I'll see what we get, but I'm betting the only prints I'm lifting from this door are Robert's," he said.

"If those tracks over there don't match any family vehicles, then I'm thinking someone met him here as he pulled up," Jett said. "What I don't get is who, and why."

"I think it looks like someone grabbed him," Tana said, surprising Jett and Shooter.

"Why's that?" Jett asked.

"The door on the truck is open and his things are inside. If it was someone he knew, he damn sure would have picked up his phone and closed the door. If those tracks don't match, they're probably from the vehicle of whoever snatched him."

They stood silently, lost in their own thoughts.

"Maybe there's something to his barge story," Tana said.

Jett snorted and looked around the farm before focusing his attention on her.

"We checked with Coast Guard—no barges on the Waterway that night, or any other for that matter," he said, firmly. "Also, even if he heard somebody, where'd they go? Or if they were getting on the barge, as he seemed to think, where the hell'd they come from?"

She felt Jett's eyes burning on her, challenging her to come up with the answers.

"You know Bobby so damn well, you tell me which of his buddies came and got him to go off without his phone, without closing the door on his truck, and without calling Alicia." She struggled to keep calm as she said this, but managed to get it out without making it sound as challenging as she meant it.

They glared at each other through the truck window.

"Hey, not my job to figure it out," Tana said, waving her hands in surrender. "That's yours. I'd hate to see you close off any avenues that might lead to Robert. It's your investigation."

Jett took a step back from the truck and inhaled deeply. He had been standing straight, with arms crossed, but relaxed and dropped his arms.

"Yeah, well, I just hate this feeling not knowing what's going on. Bobby's a good cop and one of mine—I'm damn sure going to keep anything from happening to him."

He rubbed his eyes.

"I just don't think we're dealing with a wayward accommodation barge," he quietly said. "I don't know what, but we've got too much to check into before we go off half-cocked after a boat no one else has seen."

She watched Jett as he struggled to decide how to proceed. She knew he'd handled investigations into missing children, runaway teens, even spouses making a break for freedom during a weekend getaway.

But he was getting in own way. While she knew his connection with his officers was making finding Robert harder, clouding his mind with fear and confusion, she also knew something else blocked him. Something that seemed to always block his ability to take advice, or consider her suggestions.

She noted he was quick to discount Robert's barge story after only a basic inquiry that seemed to her to miss the most obvious fact of what Robert had said: something was happening on the barge that most likely wasn't legal—why would the barge have registered the trip?

She turned and walked away, joining a group from Bougainville searching around a large vegetable garden.

As soon as she could slip away from the group, she made her way to her Jeep and quietly backed out of the driveway.

Screw Jett.

10

After leaving Robert's house, Jett returned to his office to notify County Prosecutor J.J. Johnson and Sheriff Terryman that one of his officers was missing.

No sooner had he sat down at his desk than his cell phone chirped—Shooter was calling.

"What's up?" Jett said.

"I was driving back and thought I'd check to see if there were any security cameras at the mall that might have captured Robert when he stopped in," Shooter said.

"And?"

"The GAP store has one, but they won't let me check it out until they get word from their corporate offices or we get a warrant."

"Goddamn it! I'll get a warrant right now." Jett stood up as if he was about to run out of his office for the warrant.

"OK. I thought I'd go ahead and see if there are any others along the way from where he saw Tana, at Pixie's on Old Bay Road."

"I'll send DiCicco and Hancock over to start at Pixie's. You come down Mobile Road doing the same. Let me know what you find. And tell them mall people I'll get their damned warrant."

"Right, Chief." Shooter was ready to end the call, but he heard Jett call out just before he tapped his phone. "I didn't catch that, Chief. Repeat?"

"I said tell those corporate ass lickers at the store to be ready to hand over their security tape to a very pissed-off police chief the second I get there."

Shooter chuckled. "Roger that."

After ending the call, Shooter turned to the GAP store manager, whose face had gone colorless. She must have been able to hear Jett's ranting.

"You best have that tape ready to go right away. I don't think it will be long before Chief Jeanrette gets here with a warrant."

"I...I'm sorry," the manager, a young woman somewhere in her later twenties, stammered. "I have to do what my supervisor says, and..."

Shooter turned and walked out without a word.

He climbed into his White Sands police SUV and began driving around the mall's parking area, looking for any exterior cameras. He spotted three and made notes on the locations, then texted Jett with the update.

As he drove around the lot looking, Shooter remembered one afternoon a few years ago, just after Robert joined the department and he was training Robert. He knew Robert had been in the military, and he was able to talk to Robert about policing the town while they cruised around White Sands. The two struck a friendship almost immediately, finding much in common from their days at White Sands High School, where they graduated just two years apart.

Soon, they dined out together with Alicia, and once went to New Orleans for a long weekend getaway where Shooter won $1,000 at the Harrah's Casino.

One night while cruising the downtown area, Robert said he remembered Shooter from high school, and that he looked up to the senior when he was a sophomore. He said that he thought Shooter was a "really cool," which had given Shooter a good laugh.

The memory made Shooter more determined to find Robert.

"Hang in there, buddy, I'll find the bastards who grabbed you," he said under his breath as he pulled into a parking spot at the outlet mall offices.

He went inside and told the receptionist he needed to speak to the most senior person in the office. The receptionist stood and walked down a hallway, then reappeared.

She waved to Shooter. "Sir, please come this way."

Shooter followed her down a hallway to a large office at the end. A sign on the door reported it belonged to the mall's executive director, Jason Bingham.

"Sgt. Washington, please come in," Bingham said, standing behind his desk. He dismissed the receptionist and held a hand out, indicating Shooter could sit down.

"No, thank you, Mr. Bingham," Shooter said. "I'm here in an official capacity concerning the disappearance of White Sands Police Officer Robert Gulliford yesterday. We have information that Officer Gulliford was in the GAP Store around 7:45 p.m.

"I would like to review the mall's security camera footage, if you have any, to check his movements and see if he went to any other stores."

"Oh, crap. Of course." Bingham sat down and began searching through a Rolodex on his desk. After flipping the cards in it back and forth several times, he landed on one that seemed to satisfy him. He plucked the card out and picked up his phone, dialing a two-digit extension.

Shooter heard a voice answer on the other end.

"Hi, Ron, this is Jason. We've got a police officer here who wants to review yesterday's security tapes. Says one of their officers went missing but they know he had stopped at the GAP store around seven."

He paused to listen, then covered the mouthpiece with his hand to address Shooter.

"They want to know which camera you're interested in."

"All of them."

Bingham relayed the information. A longer answer came, then Bingham hung up the phone.

"Ron—he's the head of mall security—said most of the cameras are set to record in 24-hour loops, so those cameras won't have anything from before this time yesterday."

Shooter felt his blood pressure rising.

"But he does have three cameras placed at key locations that do not erase. You're welcome to go review those."

"Great. Will it be OK for the tapes to be taken to the department for review by other investigators while I continue searching other locations?"

Bingham thought about this. He wasn't sure it was something the company had a policy about, but then decided he didn't care.

"Why don't I have Ron get them together on a thumb drive or DVD and take it to your offices as quickly as possible?"

Shooter felt like he'd gotten the first break in finding Robert. He stepped towards Bingham and stuck his hand out.

"Thank you, Mr. Bingham. We greatly appreciate your cooperation."

"I hope you find the missing officer soon and that nothing has happened to him. I have a cousin who's a police officer, so I can appreciate..."

"That's great. Thanks again, Mr. Bingham."

Shooter turned and rushed out of the office, and returned to his truck. He texted another update to Jett, who immediately responded with "Good job."

A minute later Jett texted he was on his way to the mall with the warrant for the store. Shooter chuckled, imagining the expression on the manager's face when Jett walked through the door.

Shooter left the mall and pulled into the parking area of a small strip mall across the highway. He checked the corners of the building for cameras, but didn't see any. He pulled out and then pulled back in at the next building, repeating his visual check for cameras.

Slowly, he made his way down Mobile Road, finding cameras on 14 buildings along the way. Each time he found a security camera, he checked with the property owner about recordings the police could review. Ten of the owners said their cameras were dummies, cameras placed in a visible location on the building to ward off would-be burglars and robbers.

The owner of a run-down building with a gun shop refused to say whether he did or didn't have security recording equipment.

That left three security recordings to review. Shooter arranged for all to be picked up by officers or dropped off at the department.

He headed back to the office to check in and get ready to start reviewing the recordings. When he arrived, two envelopes with thumb drives had been placed in the inbox on his desk. Gwen Brown, the department's administrative assistant, approached Shooter.

"These here are from Miles' Boats and that shopping center opposite Airport Road," she said, pointing to the envelopes. "Patrick went to get the other one from the amusement park."

She stood silently over Shooter for a moment.

"How you doing, Shooter? I know you and Robert are good friends. This must be tearing you up."

Shooter looked up at her.

"Thanks, Gwen. I'm all right—I just want to find Robert as soon as possible," he said. "Is there anyone here who can help me review these recordings?"

"No, everyone's out canvassing and looking for Robert."

"I'd like to be out looking, too, but someone's gotta review these. Can you?"

"I can, but I was thinking maybe we should get some extra help. Maybe call Tana."

"Think it'd be OK with Jett?"

Gwen turned and started back towards her desk.

"I'll just call her and see if she's got time. If she does, I'll just tell Jett she's helping and he damn well better be OK with that."

Shooter jumped up.

"Thanks, Gwen. I'm going to get back out." He jumped up and started for the door, nearly tripping in his haste to rejoin the search.

Gwen dialed Tana's number. She didn't pick up, but called back just after Gwen left a message.

"What's up, Gwen?" Tana asked.

"I wanted to see if you could help review some security videos we thought might help us find Bobby. Shooter's out trying to find out what places might have more recordings, and left me with a few hours to go through. It would really help me to have someone working on them with me while everyone's out."

Tana was silent for a minute.

"Everyone out?"

"Oh, yes, they all still out looking for Bobby."

"I can come give you a hand," Tana said. She was reluctant to go in, but couldn't turn her back on Gwen.

Twenty minutes later, she walked through the department doors with her laptop in hand. Right behind her was a large, overweight man in a white shirt emblazoned with the green flamingo logo of the Flamingo Outlet Mall above the pocket.

Gwen greeted Tana, handed her the flash drives, then turned to the man.

"Can I help you?" she asked.

"My name is Ron Dawkins," he said. "Security supervisor at the Flamingo mall. They asked me to make copies of our security tapes and bring them here."

He held out three DVDs to Gwen. She took them and thank him.

"Tana, this here's from the mall," she said, turning to Tana. "I got a disc reader on my computer— would you like me to start checking them?"

"That would be great," Tana said, without looking up as she inserted a thumb drive into her laptop. "Let me know if you have any questions."

Soon, both were silently and intently staring at the screens on their computers, tapping keys to advance or rewind the images displayed. Tana watched the recording from the boat lot, which captured little of

Mobile Road and much of the business' boats for sale lined up along the edge of the lot.

There wasn't much to see of the traffic. Tana watched carefully for a truck that looked like Robert's drive up the road. She hoped she'd be able to spot the vehicle, but the northbound traffic was barely visible in the recording.

She paid particular attention to the video for the time period between 7:00 p.m. and 7:45 p.m., when they knew Robert was at the mall. Several times, she saw trucks that she thought could be Robert's. She slowed the recording down as much as possible each time one of the trucks went by but she just wasn't sure which one was Robert, if any of them.

She had worked her way up 6:20 p.m. when Gwen let out a squeal.

"There he is! That's him," she said excitedly, pointing at her computer monitor.

Tana jumped up and rushed over the Gwen's desk. Bending over, she could see Robert driving past the parking lot camera. She noted the timestamp at the bottom of the screen—7:13 p.m.

They returned to the tedious job of crawling through the recordings, second by second, minute by minute. Since the cameras didn't always catch a clear view, they had to stop and back up the recording several times to check the images more closely.

Robert's pickup is red, but the recordings Tana was checking only recorded in black and white. Fortunately, the sporty Z-71 was distinctive enough to make it easier to spot on the videos.

She went back to the video from the boat lot. Traffic flowed and stopped, flowed and stopped—it was tedious work. After a few minutes, she watched a truck pull up and stop at the light. The truck edged forward a little as if to turn, and the driver turned towards the camera to watch the oncoming traffic.

Even from across the highway, Tana could see it was Robert. She watched as he suddenly pulled into traffic, nearly cutting off a line of vehicles crossing Mobile Road as he did.

His driving surprised her and she reached to stop the playback to rewind the recording to watch it again. It seemed out of character for Robert to drive so aggressively, and she thought maybe she'd been wrong in thinking it was him.

She reached to stop the recording. Just before her finger pressed the key to stop the video, she saw a large black SUV rushing through the intersection, as well. As she watched the SUV cut between the lanes, switching back and forth erratically and traveling much faster than the other vehicles.

She noted Robert drove by at 7:05 p.m., according to the timestamp on the recording.

Unfortunately, she could only see the vehicles travel a few hundred feet down Airport Road, but it was easier to follow the black spot of the SUV than Robert's truck.

She didn't see any more signs of Robert on the boat lot recording. When she finished, she grabbed the final DVD from the mall and popped it into her laptop.

The camera was a view from the end of one of the outer buildings towards the buildings grouped in the middle. She could see the GAP store sign across a parking lot and watched for several minutes as cars and trucks drove by in front of the stores visible on the camera's recording.

The mall video was in color and when Robert's truck pulled into view, Tana recognized it immediately. She watched as he slowly drove past and then pulled into a parking spot near the GAP store. The security timestamp recorded Robert driving by at 7:15 p.m.

She watched Robert get out of the truck and walk towards the store. Before Robert reached the door, a large SUV drove past, blocking the view of the store. When it passed, Robert had already entered the store and was out of sight.

She wondered if the SUV was the same one she'd seen on Airport Road. She rewound the recording and watched the vehicle first going backwards on her screen, then rolling through the view again.

It was a black SUV, but was it the same as the one she'd seen on Airport Road? Tana tried to see the make of the SUV, but it was hard to tell. Big SUVs are popular vehicles, and the one blocking her view of Robert didn't have anything to identify it. She studied the outline of the vehicle for a minute, then switched back to the thumb drive with the recording from the camera looking down Airport Road.

She found the SUV she'd seen before and compared what she could see of the shape of it to the SUV on the mall camera. It appeared close, but she wasn't sure.

She let the video play forward and watched as the SUV parked in a spot facing the GAP store. As she watched the vehicle's windows opened halfway, followed by a plume of smoke from someone smoking or vaping.

When the smoke cleared, she could see three men inside the

vehicle—there could be a fourth person, also, but there were definitely at least three.

She watched as the man smoking by the lowered window in the rear seat turned his head. She immediately recognized the man from the coffee shop, one of the three men who came into the shop and then immediately turned around and walked out.

Had they been following Robert? she wondered.

"Gwen, did you see a black SUV go by the videos you watched shortly after Robert went by?"

"Well, hon, I haven't been looking at SUVs. There's so many of them."

"Could you please check to see if there's a black or dark colored SUV with several men in it around the time that Robert drives by?"

"I'm checking the second DVD right now and haven't seen Robert again. I'm up 7:50 p.m. I'll switch to the other one and check it."

Gwen ejected the DVD, then inserted the first DVD she'd watched. She quickly advanced the recording to Robert driving by, then slowed down to watch the other vehicles passing the camera.

After two small, light-colored SUVs and a car drove by, a big SUV entered the view.

"Tana, I got an SUV here," she said, leaning in to her computer screen to get a closer look. "...And it looks like there's three, maybe four men inside. Less than a minute behind Robert."

Tana stepped over to her desk and took a look. Just as Gwen said, the looming SUV follows behind Robert, the shadows of two men in front and possibly two men in the back seat visible through tinted windows.

"Let's jump ahead to when Robert leaves," she suggested. "I'll check on the other camera, too."

As they resumed their search, Jett burst through the door.

"I got the store footage," he announced. "How is it going here?"

Tana stood up. Jett hadn't seen her over the high counter and stopped in surprise.

"Hi, Jett. Gwen asked me to give a hand with the videos," she said.

"Depends." He opened the swinging gate through the counter and stepper behind it. "Have you found anything?"

11

Tana reviewed everything she and Gwen had seen on the security tapes with Jett, and showed him the SUV that appeared to be following Robert.

"We were just looking for the time Robert left the mall," Tana said. "Ditto the SUV."

"Good plan. I'll check this recording from the store's system, maybe it will give us a different look."

Jett sat at a desk outfitted with the computer designated for staff use. The computer was on a system connected to county and state databases, including the Alabama Motor Vehicle Division, in addition to FBI databases.

"Let me know if you get a glimpse of the SUV's license plate," Jett said as the computer began loading and the monitor flickered to life.

All three were now closely watching the recordings. After about a minute, Gwen spoke up.

"Uh, Tana, that SUV's leaving the store but I ain't seen Robert. Check your view at 7:41."

Tana skipped ahead to the 7:40 p.m. timestamp on the video, then resumed a normal view. The SUV was already gone from view, so she rewound five minutes and restarted.

As she watched for several minutes, a steady stream of vehicles paraded by the camera. Tana never took her eyes off of the SUV on the video.

At 7:38, the SUV pulled out of the parking spot and began driving away. Tana watched carefully, hoping to catch just a glimpse of the license plate or the face of even just one man inside the threatening vehicle.

The SUV made a sharp turn in the other direction, though, and Tana didn't a chance to glean any information about the SUV or the men.

She let the camera recording continue to play, waiting for Robert to step into view on the recording.

Her wait wasn't too long: he walked out of the store with a shopping bag in hand at 7:46 p.m. She watched as Robert stepped up into his truck, pulled out of the spot and then drove back by the security camera, going back the same way he had arrived.

"Jett, do you know anyone in town who drives an SUV like that?" Tana asked.

Jett focused on his monitor and the view of Robert standing near the window display. He didn't answer for a moment.

"What? You mean a black SUV?"

"Right. Late model, black or dark—very dark—blue, maybe. It's very long, too, like the Cadillac, the Escalade."

Jett turned away from the monitor screen and rubbed his eyes.

"Sure, I know several people what's got an Escalade, dark one. Black is a pretty popular color, too."

"It's just like the ones on TV," Gwen offered. "Like the government ones, always racing through the intersections. I don't think they're Cadillacs."

"You mean a Suburban? A Chevy Suburban?" Jett turned back to his monitor.

"Yes, that's what it is," Tana said. "Thanks, Gwen. Do you know anyone who drives a black Suburban?"

"No, I don't think I do," Jett said. "The only Suburbans I see much around here belong to BODE. Their security guys drive them."

He turned to look at Tana. He could see she was working in her mind trying to add these pieces up, analyzing what pieces are missing and which ones don't fit. He could always tell when Tana was slipping into one of her "spells," as he called those times when Tana drifted away from everyone and everything around her to concentrate on some question in her mind. He had noticed when they were out on his boat about a month ago that when she slipped into a spell, her face slackened and her eyes became distant and unfocused.

"But I doubt it's them," he said after a moment. "That's kinda obvious isn't it?"

"They got no problem being obvious," Gwen pitched in. "Look how close they build them drilling rigs in the Gulf! You can't miss 'em."

Jett was watching the store video and Tana stepped over to stand behind him. Together, they watched Robert standing by the front window, taking quick looks around the store.

"What's he doing? Is he looking for someone?" she asked.

"I don't think so," Jett said. "It looks to me like he's watching the truck out the front—see, right here?" He pointed to the monitor as Robert turned his head to face the window. "He's watching them to see what they do."

"Smart guy," Tana said.

"Now when he looks around in the store, I think he's getting the layout of the place. Looking for spots where he can make a stand if he has to, or maybe an escape route."

"His training is coming in handy."

"It would be handier to have him sitting at his desk right now."

Tana absently placed a hand on Jett's shoulder and gave a squeeze.

They continued to watch as Robert milled about the store—it was after the SUV had left—and saw him select and purchase the shirt they had found in his truck earlier.

A teenaged girl came into the department just then, holding a white envelope with Shooter's name written on it. She handed it over to Gwen.

"My daddy asked me to bring this to y'all," the girl said. "Some policeman wanted our security camera recordings."

She looked at the envelope. "They in there."

Without waiting, she turned and walked out. Gwen noticed her cell phone had appeared from somewhere on her person and she was already typing furiously on it as soon as she had turned towards the door.

"I don't know where this is from but it's more security camera recordings."

"I'll take it," Tana said, reaching out for the envelope.

The envelope held a small rectangular device, colored a bright pink. Tana turned it over in her hand and saw the White Sands High School logo painted on it. It was a thumb drive and it took Tana a minute to figure out how to open it.

She inserted the drive into her laptop and opened the file with the video. The view showed a line of used cars along a busy highway. It must be Mobile Road, Tana thought. She wasn't certain what business owned the camera that captured the view, but as she watched, the black SUV appeared again.

The ominous vehicle sped past the used cars and made an abrupt turn. Tana noticed the time was 7:42 p.m.

"Jett—here's that SUV again, I think. Four minutes after pulling out of the mall."

Jett stood and came to the desk Tana was working at. He leaned low behind her to see the laptop screen.

Tana had rewound the video. "See, right here...looks like the same one, don't you think? Can you tell where this was taken?"

Jett studied the images on the screen. He thought about the different car lots along Mobile Road, which lots had the older, less expensive cars and which had newer cars. The cars on this lot were also mostly sports cars.

"I'd say that's probably Bushnell's lot," Jett said. "He sells mostly sporty cars, Camaros and Mustangs, and such."

He straightened up. "It's on the corner of Mobile Road and...crap! That's Sunset, where Robert lives."

The SUV had turned in the direction of Robert's house. If they were planning to surprise Robert, they'd have an advantage by catching him off guard at his home.

Tana quickly rewound the recording to the first shot with the SUV in view. As she slowly scrolled forward, more and more of the vehicle became visible until the vehicle's license plate was finally in view.

Tana and Jett simultaneously leaned forward towards her laptop to try to read the license plate. The vehicle's speed blurred the image, so Tana let the frames move ahead until the SUV was near the intersection.

In the recording, the brake lights brightened as the SUV slowed to make the turn. Just before the turn, Tana froze the recording and zoomed in. The license plate was clearer and she could make out three of the plate's six characters: 4, S, and K. There appeared to be a digit or letter before the three she could make out, and another group of three letters or numbers after.

And she could read "Alabama" across the top.

Jett was already back at the office desk, launching the Motor Vehicle Division database to search for the license plate.

"Tell me what you saw on the plate again." His fingers were rapidly typing: "Chevrolet" "Suburban," "black"—and when Tana gave him the characters on the plate she saw, he entered those, too.

He hit "enter" and a spinning wheel appeared on the screen while a computer somewhere in Montgomery ran through its memory chips to find any license plates matching the identifiers he entered.

It took the system about two minutes to compile a list Jett clicked immediately to print out. He ripped the long sheet out of the printer and held it up.

"We've got thirteen hits," he said. Tana watched his eyes moving across the page as he read the results. He put the list down on the desk and looked up at her.

"Two in White Sands," he said. "Leased to BODE."

12

A small spot of light was all Robert could see when he opened his eyes. He was enveloped in near-complete darkness and confusion.

He took several deep breaths to clear his head. Some kind of sedative was pulling him down, back towards sleep. To fight it, he rotated his shoulders, stretched his legs as much as possible, and flexed his back muscles. He tried to move his arms, too, but they were bound behind his back.

He would need to figure out as much as he could about where he was, then formulate a plan for getting the hell out.

His left side felt cold, chilled by the floor. It felt he was lying on the floor of some building...no, some kind of vehicle. Robert felt movement, so maybe a truck.

He took several deep breaths and listened for a moment. Not a truck, a boat of some kind. He heard the deep hum of motors and the sound of water sloshing against the sides of the craft.

With a struggle, Robert sat up. His legs were free, but numb from having not moved for a long time. How long? Could it have been more than an hour? More than a day?

As his head cleared, he remembered the last seconds before he blacked out, and his mind rewound the events leading up to the blackout: pulling up to his house, driving on Sunset Road, buying a shirt at the GAP store in the mall...and a black SUV in his rear-view mirror.

Have I been abducted?

Instinctively he knew the SUV had something to do with this, and that the SUV has something to do with the barge he saw on the waterway.

Loons, my ass.

Soon, Robert could see the faint outline of a door to the room, but he couldn't tell how much space he had around him, or if there were things on the floor nearby that would trip him. He reasoned that whoever had abducted him would soon come to ask questions, so he fought the needles of pain shooting through his legs and slid himself across the floor towards the spot of light coming under the door.

Once there, he rolled onto his knees and stood up. Leaning against the wall and working out his sore muscles, he thought about what to do next and how he might escape.

His upper chest was sore—they tased me, he remembered. That's good, he wouldn't be feeling the aftereffects for long. His left arm and shoulder hurt, bruised from his fall out of the truck.

And there was something a little sticky on the side of his face. He must have hit something falling to the ground.

Gotta tell Alicia, he thought and focused his concentration on making that happen.

He wasn't going to be able to fight back when someone came to the room with his arms tied behind him, so he tried to gauge how his captors had him trussed. The binding felt thick, more like a small rope than plastic ties, he decided.

He slid along the wall to measure the size of the room. He made it all around the room, ending back at the door when the door latch jabbed his hip. He remembered taking two steps to the first corner, four steps to the next, another two steps, then two steps before hitting the door knob.

A neat rectangular room, about six feet by eight feet. No other doors, no windows…a closet.

Robert felt around the latch to try to open the door—or at least hook the rope tying his hands on to try to cut it. The latch wouldn't budge and was too short and rounded to cut the rope.

He extended his foot, sweeping it in an arc to check the floor. Nothing there.

An empty closet.

As he leaned against the wall, voices and footsteps sounded outside the door. The sounds grew louder, then passed. It must be a hallway, and a hallway on a boat always leads to an exit.

Robert listened carefully, waiting for more people and hoping to catch a word or two of the conversations.

The sound of several heavy boots approached without anyone

speaking. The boots stopped outside the door and Robert heard keys jangling. He stepped forward and dropped to his knees. A single light overhead turned on, momentarily blinding him just before quick turns of the key and latch opened the door.

Three men stepped inside. Two men locked onto his arms while the third stepped back to watch.

"Alright, Barney Fife, let's go."

The two men nearly lifted Robert off the floor, forcing him through the door and down a hallway lined by other doors that looked like the one he'd just been forced through. The hallway ended at a "T" and the men pushed Robert to the right before pushing him through a door that led to a larger room.

He glimpsed distant lights through a door window on the shorter hallway, telling him only that it was night. He didn't get a good enough look to tell how far the lights might be, but it was clear he was somewhere offshore.

The two men dragging Robert along forced him into the single chair set up in the room, then stepped away and stood glowering at him. Robert looked the third man, clearly the leader, in the eye.

"Before we go any further, I want to check something. You do know I am a White Sands police officer, right?"

The man paused, and for a moment Robert thought he was going to ignore the question.

"Yes, I do."

"I see." That was not good. "What do you want?"

"You'll know soon enough." The man slowly stood and walked to a phone mounted on the wall, near the door. He picked up the handset and said something into it.

Robert studied the room. Like the closet he'd been in, this one was empty—or at least it looked like it had been empty until they placed the table and chair in it. The room appeared to have been unused for some time: spots of peeling paint revealed rust underneath and darkened the ceiling and walls; more rust encircled windows covered in aluminum foil along one wall.

"Hey, quick question: when does the buffet open? I'm starved." He looked around at the men, hoping to see a reaction to his comment, but was met only with their blank stares.

He would have to find a means of escaping. If these men knowingly abducted a police officer, there was little chance of them letting him go. They intended to kill him, Robert knew. Probably as soon as they found out some information they needed from him.

Robert forced himself to stay calm, taking controlled breaths. He kept his own face masked, hoping to keep his captors unaware that he knew where their plans would lead.

The third man walked back to Robert and stood behind him.

"You're a cool one, aren't you? Not a feather ruffled." The voice was harsh, but sounded like it took an effort. Robert thought of a lieutenant he'd met in Iraq named Twitles who was insecure in his command and compensated by speaking loudly to try to impress the hardened men and women in his command. His soldiers called him "Twit" but over time, it became "Twat." This guy was like that weak lieutenant, Robert decided. Lieutenant Twat.

Lieutenant Twat stepped around to Robert's right side. In a flash, he slapped Robert's right ear hard, his flat palm smashing against it. A bright flash of pain jolted Robert. His ear rang and throbbed in pain, and a small trickle of blood began running from his earlobe.

"You ruffled now, motherfucker?"

Robert steadied himself. He had experienced the temporary deafness of explosive devices blasting within feet, and the lingering ringing and pain it left in the ears. This wasn't as bad as that, but he worried the compression from the slap had ruptured his eardrum.

"What do you want?"

Lieutenant Twat stepped around to face Robert. He seemed ready to say something when the door behind him opened and closed suddenly and loudly, and rapid steps approached.

"The fuck happen to him? Why is he bleeding?"

A new voice—this must be the person in charge of this group.

"I, uh, thought he was still drowsy, so I woke him up."

Asshole.

"Get out of here. You…" Robert noticed one of the two guards who had carried him the room stiffen. "Get out, too. Go check the cargo hold."

"Yes, sir." The guard exited the room, following behind Lieutenant Twat.

"Let's try this again," the new man said in a deep, rumbling baritone voice. He stayed behind Robert and didn't step into view. "How does that sound, Patrolman Gulliford?"

Robert knew this routine. They aimed to ply him by alternating between a good guy and a bad guy. He thought about what this all added up to—their quasi-military demeanor combined with their apparent training in vehicle chases and abduction made him conclude they had some experience.

But there was something undisciplined in their actions, something not quite right. Probably not the retired pros, instead these seemed like guys who weren't able to get into the military for one reason or another, but still yearned for a military experience and training.

New-Man-in-Charge was pacing.

"Do you know where you are, Patrolman Gulliford?"

"Somewhere offshore."

"Do you know why you're here?"

"I'm guessing we're on an accommodation barge I saw on the Intracoastal Waterway make an unscheduled stop in White Sands a couple of nights ago."

The pacing stopped. "Good guessing. You can understand why…"

New Man sighed heavily. "Who did you tell about what you saw and heard?"

Robert snorted. "I'm a cop. I wrote a detailed report at the end of my shift, with a description of the barge, the location of the stop, the time you stopped, the sounds I heard. Everything. That's what police do…we check out things and write reports."

"Did you go back to where the barge stopped?"

Robert wasn't going to tell New Man about the scrap of cloth he found or the footprints there. "No."

The other guard stepped towards Robert and punched him hard on the jaw. Robert spit blood, then turned and looked at the guard to study his face.

"You're lying," New Man said. "It won't help you to lie to me."

"Won't help? Are you telling me I won't get room service tonight?"

New Man finally stepped around to face Robert. Robert looked in the man's eyes and knew this one was different—this guy was not an inept soldier-wanna-be. He had hard eyes belying years of combat.

And he was huge. His neatly-shaved head was like a tan bowling ball; the eyes were small, dark holes.

"Before we're done, we will know how much you told your chief and how far we have to go."

New Man stepped back out of view. He told the guard to wait and then left the room.

Robert waited for half a minute, then began moving his arms up and down behind his back, as if sawing against the chair frame. The guard noticed and stepped behind him to check.

When the guard bent closer to look, Robert flung his head back as hard as he could, knocking the other man down. He quickly bent forward and sprung himself up and back, holding onto the chair behind him. He landed the chair and his full weight on the guard's head.

The guard lay still—he was unconscious or worse. Robert spun around to check for a knife or something sharp on the guard's belt. Spotting a knife there, he turned and grabbed at the sheath holding the blade.

The knife fell and Robert searched for a few moments before finding it again. It was difficult, but Robert pulled the knife into his hands and slipped the tip of the blade beneath the rope.

As he pushed the knife into the rope, it stretched and tightened on his wrists. Robert could only move the knife an inch or less with each thrust, but he could feel the rope giving way.

Confident he'd soon have the rope cut, he worked his way to his feet and scrambled to the door. The knife cut through the last strands of the rope. His freed arms dropped weakly at his side and the knife fell to the floor.

Just then, the door opened, and Lieutenant Twat stepped in. He was just through the doorway when Robert raised his left leg and kicked him under the jaw with the ankle boot. The hard plastic crunched against the man's chin, sending him back against the hallway wall, where he fell in an unconscious heap.

Robert picked up the knife and stepped over the still man.

"I am ruffled now, jackass." He lifted the boot to kick the unconscious man, but stopped himself.

Instead, he turned and ran to the door leading out of the boat, pushed the door open and jumped off the deck into the water below.

Without a thought, he began swimming as fast as he could towards the lights visible on what he guessed was the shore. Robert kicked as hard as he could, but wasn't moving—the ankle boot was keeping him from fully using his foot to swim so he stopped and raised his foot out of the water to yank on the Velcro straps holding the brace on his foot.

His ankle resisted when he turned to swim again, sending painful reminders of the damaged tissue. He ignored the pain and pushed himself ahead as quickly as he could.

The barge continued moving upstream for a few minutes before Robert heard the motors shut down. After a moment of rumbling, the vessel changed direction. Robert was swimming steadily but allowed himself to look back. When he did, he saw the lights of two drilling rigs past the barge—he was in Mobile Bay.

That was good, but he also noticed something else: the boat was the barge he'd spotted two nights ago.

And it was now turning to come back towards him.

13

Robert swam as hard as was possible with his injured ankle. He adjusted his direction to swim at an angle to the shoreline. This made the swim farther, but he hoped to get ahead of the barge when it was near enough for searchlights to skim the water looking for him.

He heard the barge gaining on him and gauged the distance to the shore—it appeared he had about a hundred feet to go, but he couldn't be sure.

He redoubled his effort, pushing himself through the burning and exhaustion in his arms and shoulders, forcing his tiring limbs to work harder, push harder, move faster.

Another half a minute and he was within 30 feet of the shore. The barge sounded close, maybe a hundred feet, maybe less. He didn't risk slowing to take a look.

The shoreline had a two-foot drop he'd have to climb. Getting over the drop would expose him to the men on the barge, giving away his location and making him vulnerable to gunfire.

He glided through the shallow water, careful not to make a noise or disturb the water any more than necessary. He could hear the men on the barge—just like he'd heard them before, echoing across the water.

When he reached the shore, he rolled over. Only his head was above the water, and he could clearly see the barge.

They had turned on bright spotlights on the bow and stern of the long craft, skimming the light across the water in sweeping arcs. Robert studied their movement with the lights, and when both turned away from him, he jumped as quickly as he could out of the water.

He dove onto the ground and lay as flat as he possible. The splash he made jumping caught the attention of the men on the barge, and a searchlight flashed on the trees and palmettos over Robert's head.

Robert didn't move. He focused his attention on slowing his breathing and resting his limbs, and blocking out the throbbing from his ankle. A long night was still ahead of him, and he'd need all the energy he could muster.

After a minute, the searchlights stopped. The low rumble of the barge's motors picked up, and the craft began moving downstream.

Robert crawled through the grasses along the embankment, moving north and away from the bank. There was the possibility of coming across a snake or worse, an alligator, so he had to be ready to react quickly.

After crawling about twenty feet, Robert came to a trail running along the shore. He carefully poked his head above the brush to see where the barge was. He saw the searchlights shining across a stand of reeds several hundred feet behind him.

Feeling more confident, he stood and began a limping, lopsided jog along the trail.

The trail wound around picnic areas and wide beaches, occasionally bending into the deeper brush or stands of trees to skirt inlets and water.

After jogging about ten minutes, Robert felt exhaustion setting in. The sky was getting light, and he could see much clearer. In the daylight, he could run faster but he's also be easier to see, so for the second time he pushed himself harder. He was making good time, except for the times he turned to check the location of the barge.

A few minutes later and the barge was out of sight. Robert continued along the trail, his pace slower. On several spots where the trail was uneven, he caught a foot and stumbled a little, his still-tender ankle shooting sparks of pain.

He came across a pathway leading away from the bay and he turned to follow it. The path led to a parking lot at the end of a street. Robert walked up the street to an intersection where he could see a downtown area, a downtown area he recognized. It was Bougainville, a small town on the bay about thirty miles north and west of White Sands and only about 40 minutes away.

He could get word to Jett and be home safely in time for breakfast.

Just need to find a phone, Robert thought. He walked down the sidewalk towards downtown, then remembered a convenience store one block off Main Street on the county road. He looked around, realized the county road was in the opposite direction, and turned to walk as quickly as he could towards it.

It took him ten minutes to walk the five blocks to the store, but he found the business closed when he reached it. He walked to the end of the building, then slumped down against the wall around the side to wait for someone to arrive and open the store.

He dozed for a while. The sun was noticeably higher when he opened his eyes, but he didn't know what time it was. He peeked around the side of the store to see if anyone had arrived. The parking lot was still empty.

Robert leaned back and rested his eyes. He felt sleep and exhaustion spreading in his body, and was about to fall back to sleep, when he heard a loud vehicle approaching on the county road. He looked around the corner again to see if the vehicle came to the store. Instead of pulling in to the store, the vehicle, an old, hot-rodded Ford pickup, drove by.

Inside the truck were two men, and Robert noticed they were eyeballing the neighborhood as if looking for something.

Looking for me? He thought.

The truck drove past the store on the county road and Robert could hear the truck traveling around the small town. The vehicle's muffler must be shot, he figured, but it helped him keep tabs on its location.

Robert's attention focused on the truck, but then he heard tires on loose stones at the front of the store. He checked and saw an older man climbing out of a blue Oldsmobile. He watched as the man stepped to the front of the store and raised a hand holding a set of keys.

The noisy truck was closer now. Robert was readying himself to stand up when he spotted the Ford driving up a street two blocks away. He rolled down onto the ground and moved back from the building corner.

The loud Ford drove up and then over and then pulled into the parking lot. The driver turned off the motor and for a moment, the two men sat quietly in the truck.

"I'm looking forward to that bonus Mironoff promised," one man said. Robert crawled forward a little.

"No telling when we'll get it, though," the other man said.

Robert recognized the voice. He must have a hell of a headache, Robert thought.

The men got out of the truck and entered the store. A few minutes later, they came out with coffees and boxes of donuts in hand.

Robert listened as they got into the truck, started it up again and drove away, going back on the county road that would take them east ten miles, back to Mobile Road.

He forced himself to stand and limped his way to the door. The old man stood behind the counter.

"Morning, young fella…" He stopped mid-sentence when he saw Robert's beaten, dirty and soaked appearance.

"I need your phone to call the police." Robert slumped onto his elbows on the counter.

"This be a local call?"

"Yeah, sure." Robert rubbed the top of his head, still resting on the counter. "Local."

The man placed a dial phone on the counter next to Robert, and Robert slowly dialed Jett's cellphone.

"Hello?" Jett answered, sounding barely awake.

"Jett—it's Robert." The words came out slurred but clear enough for Jett to hear.

"Robert? Where are you? What's going on?"

"I'm at the Shop and Go in Bougainville…" He heard rustling sounds on the other end as Jett scrambled to get dressed.

"Stay there. I'm on the way."

"Jett, I was on the barge I saw. They tased me at my house, and when I woke, I was on the barge."

"Are you OK now? You sound exhausted."

"Yeah, I'm beat. I had to swim a ways in the bay getting away from the barge. They beat me a bit before I got away, and…"

"Alright, buddy. We'll get you fixed up. Hang in there—I'll be there quick as I can."

Robert slipped the phone into its cradle. He lifted his head up, and looked at the man behind the counter.

"I lost my wallet," he said, slowly and quietly. "Don't suppose I could get a coffee and roll on credit?"

14

Jett pulled on a shirt as he ran out the door. He dove into his police department SUV and launched it into gear as soon as the motor started. When he hit the gearshift into drive and stepped on the gas, the rear wheels screamed and smoked, accelerating the vehicle down the road.

At Mobile Road, he hit the siren and lights and sped north. It was eighteen miles to the turnoff for Bougainville, then another ten miles west to the convenience store, but Jett was determined to set a record for getting from White Sands to Bougainville.

As he passed Sunset Road, he couldn't help but look down the quiet lane and think about Alicia and Robert's house. He was tempted to call her, but thought he should wait and let Robert do that himself. Robert probably doesn't even know she came back home, Jett thought.

He raced through the string of little towns along Mobile Road, towns with names like Albertsville, Sundale, and Old Fort, and as he approached the turnoff, he picked up his phone and called Shooter.

"Shooter, I got a call from Robert—he's all right," Jett said as soon as the Shooter answered. "I'm picking him up in Bougainville in a few minutes."

"What happened? You sure he's all right?"

"He sounds exhausted, and we didn't get into details. I'm just passing Lambert, so I should be there in fifteen minutes or so. I'll call you as soon as I hear where's he's been."

"Thank God he's OK. Thanks for calling, Chief."

The call ended as Jett was turning off of Mobile Road, and onto the county road that would take him to the convenience store.

A few minutes later and Jett could see the store's tall sign over the road ahead. He slowed to make the turn into the store as an old pickup truck passed him going in the other direction.

Jett focused on the store in front of him and didn't notice the two men in a loud truck staring at him as they past.

He skidded to a stop at the store's front door and jumped out his truck. The sudden silence disoriented him—he expected to see Robert waiting or to come rushing out of the store, but instead everything was still and quiet.

Except for the distant noise from the pickup roaring down the county road.

Jett ran into the store, surprising the clerk stocking packs of cigarettes behind the counter.

"I received a call from a man who was here, about six two, light brown hair?"

"Yeah. He just left."

"What?"

"He left with them fellas in the pickup. You passed on the way in. I seen you."

"I don't understand, he was waiting for me."

"Well, them two came in and started talking to him, then they left."

"Talked to him? What did they say?"

"I ain't no snoop. I don't know what they said. But your friend didn't look too good. He was all beat up and dirty and wet. And when them fellers came in, he kinda looked spooked."

Jett cursed under his breath and ran back to his vehicle, again hitting the switches for the siren and lights. He gunned the motor and flew out of the store onto the county road. He was flying down the road, his truck jumping from bridge embankments and bouncing over railroad crossings.

He came over a small rise in the road and could see the pickup ahead, a mile, maybe two. Jett knew the pickup was near Mobile Road, and as he watched, he could make out the vehicle turning to head south, back towards White Sands.

Jett called Shooter again, telling him he was in pursuit of a pickup driven by two men—and that Robert was in it.

"I don't understand," Shooter said. "I thought he was waiting for you."

"Seems he got away but his captors found him and took him again. I need you to get your cruiser and come up Mobile Road. Get on the horn and get DiCicco off patrol to help, too."

"Got it. Let's get them sons-a-bitches."

Jett reached Mobile Road and turned to follow the pickup. The wider lanes on Mobile Road allowed Jett to go faster, hitting 115 mph at one point, but it didn't seem to bring him any closer to the pickup.

After passing through the wide-spot on the road known as Old Fort, Jett saw the pickup suddenly veer to the right. The vehicle was still about half-a-mile away, and he couldn't see where it went.

As he got near, he could see a dirt road turnoff the pickup must have taken, so he hit the brakes and turned the steering wheel to make the corner.

His top-heavy SUV leaned and nearly toppled over as he cornered too sharply on the loose dirt, but then abruptly righted itself and he again hit the gas. He drove three miles without seeing the pickup, when the dirt road ended in the middle of a field of cotton plants.

He spun around and headed back. Either he'd taken the wrong turn or the pickup pulled off somewhere along the way and he'd passed it.

He slowed down a little, watching for possible hiding spots on the way back to Mobile Road. An old wooden building seemed like it could be a place for the truck to hide, but Jett didn't see any tracks the pickup would have left in the brush if they'd pulled off the road.

He got back to Mobile Road as Shooter was racing up on the other side of the divided road. Shooter slowed and maneuvered the Charger across the road to pull up alongside Jett.

"Where'd they go?" Shooter called out to Jett.

"I lost them somewhere around here— I think they pulled off but I don't know where."

Shooter looked up and down the highway.

"I think there are a couple of turnoffs coming up down the road they might'a taken. Patrick will be here soon and we can check them out."

"I'll continue on and see if I can spot them." Jett hit the gas again and took off down Mobile Road towards White Sands.

Shooter pulled around and drove to a cutoff from the road located a few hundred feet away but hidden by a tall hedgerow. He called to Patrick and directed him to a second cutoff from the highway.

Jett was a mile-and-a-half ahead now. He was driving slower to keep an eye out for the pickup truck, but he didn't see any signs of it. Shooter radioed to him that neither he nor Patrick saw the pickup.

15

Tana rolled over in her bed and stretched. She reached for her cell phone to turn off the alarm set to wake her at 6:30 a.m.

As she lay in bed, her mind picked up a thread of thought she'd been mulling over and over before falling asleep: what would an oil drilling services company be doing on the waterway? She had considered more than fifteen different possible reasons for the company to run a barge up the waterway, from transporting a crew of workers from an oil rig to renting the barge for a company event.

Just before nodding off, she was asking herself which of those reasons would cause the company to go after Robert?

She woke with two reasons for that in her mind: the barge was being used to transport illegal workers or illegal materials.

As she rose and dressed for a short run, her mind kept working on what this meant and what she could do to check if either was, in fact, the cause of Robert's disappearance.

She opened the kitchen door at the back of the house and stepped out onto the little stone patio in the shade of her backyard. With an arm raised above her head, she stretched to her right side, keeping her eyes fixed on the tall grasses that grew on the other side of the trail at the end of her yard. She remembered the dead body of Joey Beaumont in those grasses, the look of terror fixed forever in Joey's eyes when Tana shot her.

But even as she recalled all that had happened in the spring, her mind was still turning ideas over and over, like tumblers in a lock, until falling into place with the right combination. She was considering all the pros and cons of her ideas to check up on BODE and any activity on the waterway.

She had several ideas, including putting some cameras somewhere on the canal, that she was developing as she finished stretching her back, arms and legs, and took the first few steps. She slowly jogged around to the front of the house and onto the street pavement. She had been running a circuit that took her up to Old Bay Road, then a mile west towards the bay before turning back and running to Mobile Road and a final turn taking her back home.

The morning air was a little thick with humidity, but cool and comfortable. The humidity caused her to be unnaturally soaked after running the first mile, but by that time she had sped up and was almost sprinting down the sidewalk along Old Bay Road.

She was on the way back, a block from Mobile Road, when she watched as a noisy, old pickup truck raced past on Mobile Road. She heard the scream of a police car siren in pursuit, and when it passed on Mobile Road, she recognized it as Jett's SUV.

What is Jett doing chasing speeders so early? Tana wondered.

She reached Mobile Road and watched as Jett continued down the road, about two hundred feet behind the truck. As she watched the truck suddenly skidded to a stop, swerving to the left and coming to a stop blocking the lane.

She saw two men jump out of the truck and raise long guns towards Jett. The guns began firing and Tana recognized the sound as being from either an M4 or AK-74, military-grade automatic weapons.

"Jett!" she screamed as Jett slammed his brakes. She began running towards him—and the shooters—without thinking, but when she reached the end of the block, just a few hundred feet from the shooting, stray bullets whizzed overhead and she dove behind a brick wall separating a bank from a small office building next door.

As she listened, she heard a new sound: the full-throated blast of the shotgun mounted in Jett's SUV. The shotgun fired three rapid shots in answer to several short bursts from the automatic guns, then two more.

There was a quick burst from the shooters, then Tana heard the loud motor of the truck startup.

She peered around the edge of the wall and saw the truck turn to drive away. And Jett on the ground.

She stood and sprinted as fast as she could to Jett. When she got to his side, she could see blood darkening his back above his left shoulder.

He moved and Tana reached down to help him turn over.

"Get me up," he said, raising his right arm to Tana. She grasped his hand and his arm and pulled. He stepped toward the open door of the SUV. "Get in—they've got Robert."

Tana ran to the other side of the vehicle and climbed up. Two other police cars were speeding towards them now.

"Jett, you're shot."

"Not shot enough." He turned the key to start the truck, but nothing happened. "We've got to get them and find Robert."

He turned the key again, but the SUV wouldn't start. A cloud of smoke drifted out from under the hood.

Shooter and Patrick stopped, and as Shooter was getting out of his car, Jett called out to him.

"Go get them—they turned west on Gulf Highway." He waved his right arm frantically, signaling them to go.

Both of the cars raced off again, and Jett and Tana watched as they turned on Gulf Highway.

Jett picked up his radio handset. "Hancock, this is Jett."

"Go ahead, Chief."

"I need an ambulance sent to…" He looked around at the storefronts for an address number. "…to 1053 Mobile Road."

Tana looked around for a first aid kit and spotted one in the back of the SUV. She jumped out of the truck and retrieved it as Jett told Hancock he would need a tow truck, as well.

She grabbed a strip of gauze and roll of tape and stepped to the driver's side door. Jett was half-in the vehicle, leaning forward slightly.

"Can we get that shirt off your shoulder so I can take a look?"

Jett moved his arm slightly and winced. "I don't think so."

"OK." Tana held up scissors from the kit and began cutting the shirt from the bottom up.

"Hey—hold on there."

Tana stopped cutting and looked at Jett.

"This was good shirt…" he half-smiled.

"You know, you're about half an inch from having a really bad day," she said. "Pretty damn lucky you weren't killed."

"Robert said he was on the barge he'd seen on the waterway. He said he got away but these guys in the pickup caught up with him in Bougainville."

"Did he know what they want? Seems pretty insane to abduct a police officer."

"No, we didn't get that far. He called from the Stop and Go and I headed out as fast as I could."

Jett gazed down the roadway. "I'll kill those assholes. I swear, anything happens to Robert…"

Tana had cut the shirt to the collar and was gently peeling it off of the bleeding shoulder. Two bullets had struck Jett, one hitting high and going all the way through the muscle. The other was a little lower and did not go through his body but stopped somewhere inside his upper chest.

She placed a piece of the gauze on the exit wound from the bullet when she heard the siren of an ambulance. Looking up, she saw the vehicle turn onto Mobile Road and head towards them.

16

An ambulance flew by the old truck on Gulf Highway, making its way to Jett.

"That was fucking close, man," the driver said. "I don't know why Mironoff is so concerned about this guy that we should take on the whole fucking police department."

The man sitting next to him grunted. He slumped against the door.

"Ben? You OK?" The driver reached over and pushed on his partner's shoulder, which made his left arm shift to reveal a large blood-stained spot on his side.

"Shit." The driver slowed a little, and shifted his body to the right, so that he was almost sitting in the middle of the truck's bench seat. He gripped the steering wheel firmly in his left hand, then extended his right arm as far as he could. With a quick motion, he jerked open the door latch and pushed the other man out of the truck.

The truck veered to the right just enough for the rear wheels to slam against the man's upper torso, ending whatever bit of life was left in his body.

The driver moved back to his seat behind the wheel and hit the gas to push the truck faster. Two blocks up, he turned to the right, then spun into a parking lot next to a boarded-up, two-story hotel building. At the back of the building was a garage and shop that he pulled the truck into before closing the doors.

He stood listening at the door, hearing the rising wail of police cars as they approached on Gulf Highway, then fading as the cars raced further to the west. When the cars were sufficiently far away, he turned his attention back to the truck.

Robert lay inside the box, legs bound, arms held behind his back by plastic ties. A thick black hood covered his head. He was motionless.

The driver jumped into the box and gave Robert a kick. Robert didn't react. He reached down and yanked the hood off Robert, then frantically looked over Robert's head, body and legs for blood–the shooting pockmarked the truck with several holes, and the man worried Robert had also been shot.

The only blood was on the top of Robert's head, and it wasn't enough for a serious injury.

The man gave Robert's leg another kick.

"Wake up, asshole."

Robert stirred. As his eyes fluttered before opening, the man yanked the hood back over his head.

"You cost us a lot today, jackass. Mironoff's going to take it out of your hide, I'd guess."

He jumped out of the truck and grabbed Robert's legs, pulling Robert almost off the truck. He walked over to the back wall of the shop and unlatched a wide, swinging door. The door opened onto the lagoon, and a small dock connected to the shop building. A small, flat boat tied to the dock bobbed slightly on the water.

The man walked back to Robert.

"Listen here. I'm putting you in a boat. Give me any shit and I'll drop your carcass in the water. You ain't treading water with your legs and arms tied up, so you can sink and drown for all I care."

He lifted Robert. "You feel me?"

Robert grunted.

The man hoisted Robert half over his shoulder, then negotiated his way down two wooden steps to the dock, and one to the boat. He bent forward and carelessly dropped Robert into the boat. He untied the boat, stepped into it, and started the motor.

After pushing away from the dock, he turned the boat towards the west. As the boat slowly gained speed in the water, he reached down and lifted a fishing pole.

Anyone looking out at the lagoon would see an early morning a guy making his way to a favored spot for fishing.

The boat hummed along to the far western end of the lagoon. It slowed and wove in and out of stands of reed growing at the water's edge.

When he found the clearing through the reeds he was looking for, the driver motored the boat in, letting it slide to a stop on the lagoon's sandy shore. The driver then stepped out into the shallow water and pulled the boat aground until it was safely out of the water.

He stood and looked around.

"Damn it."

A moment later, he heard a vehicle driving slowly in his direction. It pulled into a clearing and stopped. Two men dressed in khaki-colored parachute pants and black T-shirts stepped out.

"Where's Ben?"

"Side of the road, back by the Quickmart."

"Alive?"

The driver snorted. "Well, Hotshot, I doubt it. Took one in the abdomen, then got hisself in the truck's way when he fell out."

"Jesus. Where is the cop?"

"Right here." The driver nodded in the boat's direction, and the two men walked down to the waterline. They reached in and pulled Robert from the boat. As they cleared the water, Robert began jerking and twisting, causing the man holding his upper body to drop him.

Robert's head hit the sand with a dull thud and he groaned through the hood covering his head.

The men looked at each other and laughed.

"All right, all right, let's get him to the bay," Hotshot said.

The three of them lifted Robert and carried him to the back of the SUV Hotshot had driven to the side of the lagoon. They put him down in the back of the vehicle, then all got in and drove away.

17

After the ambulance left with Jett, Tana ran back to her house and quickly washed and changed. She drove to the medical center and asked the woman at the front desk where she could find Jett.

The woman tapped on computer keys, then stopped to read the results of her search.

"We have a Michael Jeanrette just admitted to surgery for…ooh, my, gunshot wounds?" She looks up at Tana. "Is it serious?"

"I hoped you could tell me," Tana said. "I don't think so, but I don't really know."

"You can go to the waiting room for surgery on the second floor of the west wing." She picked up a map of the medical center and drew a few lines to show Tana how to negotiate her way to the waiting room in the labyrinthine hospital.

Tana snatched the sheet and rushed down the hall, trying to match the map with the inscrutable hallway markings and signs. "Why is every damn hospital in this country built like a medieval keep?" she mumbled after making a wrong turn before stopping at a door marked "Maternity." She consulted the map again, looked back and saw the doorway she needed to go through to get to the elevator banks which would take her to the second floor of the center's west wing.

As the elevator lifted her, Tana was embroiled in emotions. She was more than just concerned about Jett; she felt a need to nurture and be supportive to him, even though she didn't know why. Jett had hurt her, or maybe she hurt Jett, she couldn't remember right now, but either way, her feelings for him confused her.

When the door opened on the floor, Tana saw a large open area with

TVs, tables and various chairs and sofas around. About a dozen people were waiting in the room, including Shooter and Pat DiCicco and Tana rushed over to them.

"Shooter–any word?"

"Hey, Tana. They said he'll be fine," Shooter said. "Both shots missed any vitals, but one chipped some bone from his craver…"

"No, his clavicle," DiCicco corrected, grinning. "His collar bone."

"Right, right, collar bone. Anyways, they said they need to remove the one bullet that didn't go through, clean the wounds, and bandage him up."

Tana released her breath and relaxed. "Good, good," she said. She looked down and sighed again, then looked up at DiCicco. "So, what happened? I only saw him racing down Mobile Road in pursuit when those guys opened fire on him."

"He got a call from Robert, said he was on his way to pick Robert up in Bougainville," Shooter said. "But when he got there, the guys in the truck had taken him. We…" he jerked a thumb towards DiCicco, "were trying to find them up off of Mobile Road, when Jett radios and says he's chasing them down in town."

"It was all over by the time we got there, though," DiCicco said.

Tana walked to a table and slumped down in it. She started laying out the pieces in her head: Robert turns up in Bougainville, calls Jett, then gets kidnapped again.

"Did Robert say anything about what had happened?"

"All Jett told me was Robert said he was kidnapped but got away," Shooter said. Tana could see by DiCicco's expression he didn't know even that much.

"Didn't say by whom?"

"No, but I got a good idea who and I'm going to track those fuckers down."

"I don't get it," Tana said. "We're thinking it's got something to do with the barge he saw, right? And we're thinking that barge has something to do with BODE, right?"

"Yes and yes," Shooter said, sliding into a chair opposite Tana.

"So the guys in the hot-rodded, beat up old truck are working for BODE? And they figured it made sense to snatch Robert again, then turn Mobile Road into the OK Corral? Start shooting at a chief of police?"

"Well, I s'pose they didn't know he was chief…just a cop in their way," Shooter said.

"Where would they be taking Robert?"

"I don't know. The truck turned west on Gulf Highway and we tried to catch up. Didn't find them, so they pulled off somewhere. Mighta pulled off to put Robert on a boat on the lagoon or the bay inlet."

DiCicco nervously held his hat in his hands, pinching the creases and turning it over and over. He stood otherwise silently, with an expression that showed both worry and fear.

Tana watched him for a moment.

"You OK?" she asked.

"I've never seen a gunfight before—never thought I'd see something like that, middle of the street, broad daylight…in White Sands," he said quietly. "These guys had automatic weapons—and they kidnapped a police officer. What's this world coming to? How can I go home and tell my fiancee about this?"

Tana looked at Shooter, trying to read his thoughts. He was thinking the same thing, how this changed everything about being a cop in White Sands. If there are people desperate enough or violent enough to do this, what's next? Was White Sands becoming "No Place for Old Men?"

She was trying to find something to say to comfort them, maybe a relatable anecdote from her experience in St. Louis, but nothing came to mind. Before she could come up with an answer, a doctor in scrubs walked through a pair of double doors leading to the surgery ward and looked around. Upon seeing the two officers, he walked to them.

"I trust you people are here for Chief Jeanrette," he said, reaching out to shake everyone's hands and adding his name was Jones. "I performed the surgery on Chief Jeanrette. It was pretty minor as these things go. We got the bullet out from deep tissue in his upper chest and have him patched up. He lost a good amount of blood, but otherwise, he's very lucky. He's in recovery right now. I'd like him to stay put for a few hours before anyone starts on him, if that's possible."

"Did you give him any horse tranquilizers?" Shooter said. "If you didn't, I doubt you'll keep him still for any length of time."

"We didn't knock him out or anything. I told him—and I'm telling you—he can leave any time *after* we do a post-op in an hour. Until then, he's trapped in recovery without a phone, so I hope he can be still for just a bit."

With that, the doctor turned and went back to the ward.

"Are you going to wait here, Tana?" Shooter asked. "DiCicco needs to go check out at the station, but I can give Jett a ride back."

Tana sat quietly for a moment. She was staring at the table in the blank way she did when getting lost in thought, so Shooter just waited for a response. He'd seen her do this enough to know it's just part of her personality.

It took almost a full moment for Tana to realize what Shooter had asked. She looked up, surprised he even asked. Of course, he didn't know how she was feeling towards Jett, though he'd probably sensed it at times in recent weeks.

"I'm...I think I'll...," Tana stammered while rising slowly from the chair. Suddenly, she looked up at Shooter. He could see the intensity in her eyes that she had when she closed a gap in ideas, or made a determination about something. "I'm going to get going."

She turned before either Shooter or DiCicco could say anything and rushed to the elevator.

"Dang!" DiCicco said. "What was that about?"

18

An hour later, Tana was watching traffic on Canal Road from the picnic table where she believed Robert had taken his coffee break. Her mind was rewinding the information she had about Robert's sighting of the barge. She stood and began walking down the path towards where Robert said the barge had stopped.

After walking about a half mile, she stood and looked at the water in the Intracoastal Waterway, and the shoreline opposite. If she was in the right place, she could have a clear, unobstructed view of anything happening across the waterway—unless the barge blocked the sight line, which it probably did.

As she studied the area across the waterway, movement from someone approaching her on the path caught her eye.

A tall, thin Black man in standard Coastal attire—a colorful short-sleeved shirt and knee-length shorts—was walking along the path, looking at trees and birds across the waterway. Tana figured he was an out-of-town visitor enjoying a stroll, but when he stopped at her side and turned to follow her gaze across the water, she wondered what he was up to.

He looked at Tana again.

"You seen her, too?" he said after a pause.

"What?" Tana turned to face him. He was much older than she had thought—and also clearly not a visitor. The man wore an ancient shirt and stained and tattered surfer shorts, every cuff and seam fraying.

"The warblers? There's always some cute little warblers over there."

"No, I'm not bird watching."

"Oh." He stood silently, studying Tana's face.

"You seen the barge?" he asked quietly after a moment. "I don't know what they doing but it ain't fittin'. I gets to worrying every time that barge come."

"You've seen the barge? How often?"

"Oh, I don't know. It comes up here about every few days, I guess. Middle of the night."

He turned towards the road and pointed towards a string of little shops across the road.

"That's my baby girl's place, over there. I like to keep an eye on her, so I come by most every night." He dropped his arm, and his face fell. "She won't see me no more, though. So I got to just come keep an eye on her."

Tana looked across the street. At first she thought he pointed to one of the shops, but then she noticed a taller building, likely an apartment building, rising past the stores.

She looked back at the man, studying his face to estimate how helpful his information might be.

"Tell me about the barge."

"Oh, the barge. It been coming here about a month now. Always stops right here. Then I hear noises. Don't like the noises."

"The 'noises?'"

"Yeah. Sounds like a bunch of people moving around, like some kids or something, sniffling and making sounds like they crying. Then a bus comes. That's after the plane lands. Big old plane." He swept his arm across the sky and looked up as if tracing the path of the plane.

Tana wondered if the stranger was making sense. He appeared homeless, and it's possible a mental health issue was behind his current situation and relationship with "baby girl."

"So…you're saying a bus comes down here and meets the barge?"

"And it leaves. Just about every couple of days."

"When did you last see it?"

"Uh, couple nights ago…I think." His face clouded with confusion for a moment as he tried to recall what day it was. A bird called out across the water, and he suddenly looked in the direction of the sound, smiling. "There she is."

He looked at Tana's confused face.

"That's a Hooded Warbler. She's a pretty little thing." He turned back, looking for the bird.

"So, you saw this barge two nights ago. Did you hear anything when it stopped?"

"I heard lots. There was some policeman right here, chasing them.

Never seen that before. He fell down right over there."

So everything Robert reported was correct—and if the bird man was correct, the barge would likely be back tonight.

"My name's Tana. What's yours?"

"I'm Spence." He turned to face Tana and made a small bow. "Always nice to make the acquaintance of a fine woman, Miss Tana."

"Where do you live, Spence?"

Spence was still looking for the bird.

"Oh, you know, I move about some. Kinda live here and there."

Tana remembered a coffee shop on Canal Road within walking distance.

"Can I buy you a coffee and a roll? I'd like to hear more about this barge and…"

Spence froze, suddenly. "Oh, no, thank you, Miss Tana. I can't go to the coffee shop. You shouldn't go, neither. There's some bad people there. Sometimes."

"Bad people? You mean, people who are mean to you?"

"No. Bad. I mean people I seen on that barge."

Spence suddenly became excited. "There she is, there's my little warbler." He pointed at a tree across the waterway, and when Tana looked, she saw a few quick flashes of yellow and green in the lower branches. The small bird flew out of the tree towards another branch on a tree about a hundred feet back on the canal. "Ain't she a beauty?"

Spence turned and held out his hand. "OK, then. I gotta be going—warbler's going to get away. It was nice to meet you, Miss Tana."

He started walking down the path again.

"Wait. Can I talk to you again? Where can I find you?"

Spence spun around without missing a step, walking backwards on the path. He was smiling brightly. "Oh, I'm always here on the path, watching for warblers and such. You just come here and you'll find me. Goodbye."

He waved and turned back around, leaving Tana standing on the path.

She looked back across the water. The tree the warbler had been in was next to a narrow cut through the underbrush leading away from the water. She studied the area and could see a row of trees leading from the waterway in a neat row towards the airport.

If Robert found something, he found it over there.

She turned and studied a tree next to the path, about twenty feet away. She had been wondering if would be possible to observe the barge landing, and she realized it wouldn't take a great height to see over the barge. If the barge did block the view of the activity, a quick climb to even the lowest branch would make for a much better view since the waterline was nearly ten feet below the embankment on this side of the waterway. A climb higher could be even more unobstructed.

An idea was taking hold in her mind. She wasn't certain it would work. There were still too many questions—but some of those questions could be answered by getting a closer look at the clearing where the barge is landing.

She drove back to Mobile Road and crossed the bridge, then turned on Airport Road. She passed the airport and continued driving, missing the narrow road which led to the canal. When she reached the stop sign at the White Sands Beach Bypass, she realized she'd gone too far.

She drove more slowly, looking for roads, paths, tracks or anything leading off the road. The only one she came to was a paved road leading to the monstrous BODE facility.

"Screw it," Tana said, and cranked the Jeep into a hard left. She followed the road, passing the security gate at BODE. The pavement ended several hundred feet past the entrance, but she continued on the rough dirt surface. Tana noticed a row of Drake Elm trees ran from the point where the pavement ended to the waterway.

As the waterway grew close, the road ended.

Tana stepped out of the Jeep. The bare dirt was hard packed and baked by the Alabama sun. To her right was a high chain-link fence, topped in razor wire. BODE, Tana figured.

To her left was a path through the elms. She walked down the path, through the trees, and into the large clearing.

Tana stepped slowly towards the waterway, feeling the air becoming more humid near the warm water. She spotted the path leading from the clearing to the waterway and scanned the area for tracks or debris or anything to support Robert's claim.

She turned back towards the clearing. It could just be the party spot for local high schoolers, or a campsite for someone fishing in the waterway.

As she looked across the clearing, a light flashing in a tree caught her attention. Stepping towards the tree, she saw the flashing was a small, red light. On a security camera.

Tana turned around to imagine the camera's view.

Why would someone put a security camera here? Catch kids partying? Trespassing fishers to prosecute?

She turned and started back towards the waterway when a large pickup truck barreled into the parking area, sliding to a stop just inches from her Jeep.

Two men jumped out and jogged towards Tana.

"Hold it, ma'am," a short stocky man with reflective blue sunglasses said. Tana studied the man. He'd struck a pose intended to convey authority, but she really only noticed how his ears stuck out from the side of his head. Did his sunglasses cause that or was just the way the man's ears are?

Either way, it undermined his attempted projection of authority.

The other man placed himself at Tana's left, silently.

"This is private property," Big Ears said. "You're trespassing."

Tana studied his manner. He was standing confidently, but with his legs close together.

Quiet Man, however, stood straight and still, legs shoulder-width apart and braced to react quickly. She turned her head and looked at the quiet man, locking her gaze on his face as if she was seeing through his sunglasses. He was in charge of this duo and conveyed more skill at dealing with trespassers than Big Ears.

"I see. As it happens, I was just leaving."

She took two steps towards her Jeep, when Big Ears rushed up to her and grabbed her arm.

"I need to see your identification." A bead of sweat rolled down his cheek.

"Why?" Tana was calm, and watched sweat gathering on his face.

"You're trespassing and we will prosecute."

"Let go of my arm. I told you I am leaving."

"I need your identification."

The man held her left arm firmly.

"Are you posing charges?"

"That's not for me to decide, but I need to see your identification."

"Then call White Sands police. I'm not giving you my name."

Big Ears looked to the other, seeking guidance.

"And let go of my arm now," Tana said.

She'd said it loudly, wanting to alert Quiet Man that she wasn't intimidated by them. Then she quietly added, "I'll give you to the count of five to let go."

Big Ears' eyebrows jumped up. "Miss, I need to…"

"One…"

He looked again for direction from the other man.

"Two…"

When she reached four, Big Ears stepped to twist her arm behind her. Tana expected the move and spun around before he could react. In a second, she was free from his grip and standing face to face with him, his surprised face in front of her.

She gave him a quick smile, then kneed the man squarely between his legs. He dropped to the ground, groaning.

Quiet Man watched as his partner fell, then raised his eyes to Tana. She was staring at him, waiting for his next move. Her right arm relaxed at her side, but held her pistol.

"I'm leaving now, as I said before." She slowly stepped around Big Ears, who was rolling on the ground, clutching his groin. She backed her way to her Jeep without taking her eyes off of Quiet Man.

Once inside, she started the engine, and gunned it as she slammed the gearshift into drive. The Jeep jumped and spun around, then zipped back down the road ahead of a billowing, brown cloud of dust.

Tana kept her eyes on the rear-view mirror, watching for the truck. But even as she sped past the security gate at BODE, no one was following her on the road.

She called Jett, but he didn't pick up—she figured he's still in the recovery room, sans cellphone and not able to answer. She thought about calling Shooter, but then had a better idea.

Maybe she could turn the tables on whoever is watching the activity at the clearing. When she reached Mobile Road, she turned right to head north. In less than an hour, she was driving on Highway 90 in Mobile.

19

Robert tried to keep track of the turns and distances traveled, but it was hard with the hood blocking his view of any familiar landmarks. For a while, he could pretty much tell where he was just by bumps in the road and traffic sounds.

He followed the route taken in his head, guessing the SUV drove up West Oyster Beach Drive in White Sands, then turned left onto Old Bay Road. Even though he felt disoriented riding on the floor in the back of the vehicle, he could tell they were following Old Bay Road because the road is almost perfectly straight. He visualized the journey on the length of the long peninsula that jutted out between the Gulf and Mobile Bay.

At the end of the peninsula, next to an old fort built to protect the bay from Union ships during the Civil War, was a small ferry launch to Dauphin Island on the opposite side of the bay. Robert listened as the ferry's diesel motor rumbled through the quiet morning air, then noted the slight bobbing the ferry made on water as the SUV chugged its way.

The three men got out and stood silently on the deck, watching the water as the ferry crossed the bay entrance.

After reaching Dauphin Island, the SUV crossed over to the main land on the Dauphin Island Parkway. Robert knew they had traveled through the Island, and kept track of their movements across the Parkway, but as they drove up to Alabama Port, he lost track of the turns and stops.

The SUV turned on Highway 188 towards Bayou Le Batre and from there, traveled on to Pascagoula, Mississippi. They passed through Pascagoula to a warehouse on the northwest side of the city built along the Pascagoula River.

Hotshot drove and backed the SUV up to a landing dock at the warehouse. Robert felt the change in direction and the slow backing, knowing they were at their destination. He prepared himself for another attempt to exit and free himself at any chance he could find.

The SUV came to a stop, and the men exited. They gathered at the rear of the SUV; Robert listened to the low voices moving around the vehicle.

When Hotshot opened the SUV's rear door, Robert kicked his legs out, attempting to connect with someone. But his legs only kicked through the air, missing the men completely.

"Quiet him down, would you, Eight Ball?"

The man called "Eight Ball" had driven the old truck and had brazenly wielded a Heckler and Koch HK-416 on Mobile Road in the middle of White Sands. He was the one who threw his partner from the truck, and Robert into the boat. He reached in and yanked Robert into a sitting position. He pulled the hood tight, revealing the outline of Robert's head and face.

Then he gave Robert a hard right to his face, just below Robert's left eye, and Robert crumpled in a heap.

"How's that? Quiet enough for you, Hotshot?"

He and the third man picked Robert up and carried him to a door.

"Take him to the lunchroom," Hotshot said. "Mironoff wants to talk to him."

Robert woke with a start. His head pounded, even more so when he opened his eyes. The room's lights seemed blinding after the time he'd been in darkness under the hood and the time he'd been unconscious.

As his vision cleared, he looked around the room. It was a company lunchroom, devoid of personality, decoration, or windows. It did have an aging refrigerator, sink, and microwave with grease oozing out around the door.

He was tightly bound to the chair; it seemed they remembered the last time they had him tied up and would not repeat the mistake. Robert was completely unable to move.

But he could open his mouth, so he took in a deep breath and let out a howl.

That should rouse them. Whatever this is, let's do it.

A minute later, Robert heard footsteps, too many to count, approaching the door, which then slammed open as five men entered.

All except one lined up in front of Robert, dressed in what he viewed as their uniform: olive green parachute pants, black T-shirts, combat boots. He snorted. Wannabes.

"Thank you for coming to the meeting," Robert said, giving them a smirk. He recognized the man on the left as one of the two men who forced him out of the convenience store in Bougainville and into the back of their truck. He took a step towards Robert.

"Get back, Eight Ball." That deep voice from behind him. A moment later, Mironoff stepped around and stood before Robert. This time, he was dressed in business casual, looking tanned and relaxed. He played nice cop last time Robert was on this barge and Robert figured they were done with that routine.

"So, boss, what's happening?" Robert said. He hoped to antagonize them, maybe they'd make a mistake he could turn to his advantage.

"See, Mironoff? The guy's a pain in the ass," Eight Ball said. "When the time comes, let me finish him."

Mironoff turned and glared at Eight Ball.

"Shut. The. Fuck. Up." Eight Ball shrunk back. Mironoff stepped towards Robert. "That's pretty funny. 'What's happening?'"

The other men formed a ring around the chair.

"What's happening is I think you're a problem I have to address. I think you're bad for business."

"What business is that? Running drugs? Human trafficking?"

"Who did you tell about the barge?"

"Did Crazy Eight over there kill my chief?"

"I don't know. Don't care, either."

Mironoff bent down to Robert's face. "Who did you tell? I'll wipe your entire fucking department, if I need to. You can save a lot of people a lot of pain if you'll just tell me."

Robert looked around at the other men. They actually might try to take on the whole department, he thought. Crazy looking bunch— especially Eight Ball.

"Hey, Eight Ball—what unit were you in?"

Eight Ball glared at him, and he didn't answer.

"Oh. Couldn't cut it. I'm sorry—that must still sting." Eight Ball's eyes widened just a bit, enough to confirm Robert's suspicion.

Mironoff grabbed a handful of Robert's hair, holding his head while swinging a hard left into the back of his head. The punch landed just below where he'd hit his head in the boat. Robert nearly passed out. The sounds of the room dimmed and his vision grew dark but not quite all the way to black before returning.

He looked up at Mironoff, his eyes taking a second to focus.

"Sandy Basko know about this?"

Mironoff squinted. Why did this man mention Basko?

"I've got other things to do," he said, turning towards the door. As he held the door open before exiting, he looked back. "Just remember what I said."

Mironoff left the room, and the men huddled closely over Robert.

"You guys got any sandwiches? I'm hungry as hell after escaping last night."

"Not a problem," one man said, his voice cold and flat.

20

Jett sat on the edge of the hospital bed, his left leg shaking. He rubbed his forehead with his right hand while his left arm remained tethered to an IV bottle hanging from a pole at the head of the bed.

When a nurse walked into the room, he jumped up.

"I gotta go. Will you please remove this?" he said, tugging on the tube.

"I can't do that, Mr. Jeanrette. Not until the doctor says so."

"Then get the damn doctor in here. I...have...to...go, *now*."

He was red-faced, and the combination of strong words and his bulk scared the nurse. She turned and dashed out the door.

In a few minutes, the nurse returned in the shadow of a doctor who appeared to Jett to be far too young to have completed any college, let alone medical school.

"Is there a problem, Mr. Jeanrette?"

"Yes, there is, and I need you to get me out of here ASAP so I can find the sons-a-bitches who shot me and kidnapped my officer."

The doctor looked down at a clipboard in his hands, reading through and flipping the pages. He jotted a few lines at the bottom and handed the clipboard to the nurse.

"I'm not prepared to release—"

Jett grabbed the IV tube on his left arm and pulled it out. He calmly walked over to the pile of his clothes and began dressing.

"Sir, please, you can't just..."

Jett jerked around, glowering at the twenty-something doctor.

"Well, I just fucking did and now I'm leaving. I don't have time to..."

He suddenly stopped and looked down where his feet were

struggling to find the legs of his pants. His needed his left arm to reach down and pull his pants up, but the arm was out of commission at the moment.

He sighed and sat back against the bed.

"Doctor, I have a police department under attack, with a missing officer. I can't...I have to get out there to find him."

The doctor studied him for a moment, then turned to the nurse.

"Jeanine, please get a dressing on Mr. Jeanrette's arm and get him out as quickly as you can."

He turned his attention back to Jett as the nurse left the room to gather bandages.

"Please understand we need you back here at your first opportunity to check the shoulder. If you don't, you will risk having limited movement in the arm. Permanently."

"I get it, doctor, really I do." Jett had the right leg of his pants past his knees; the left leg was caught under his foot. "I wouldn't act this way if it really wasn't necessary."

"Let me give you a hand."

They were pulling Jett's shirt over his injured shoulder as the nurse entered with a small bean-shaped tray filled with cotton gauze, bandages, scissors and other materials. Jett held his arm out as far as he could, a grimace flashing on his face as he moved the arm, and the nurse quickly wiped the red spot on his forearm with an alcohol wipe before applying a bandage.

Together, the nurse and doctor helped Jett finish dressing, and as soon as his shoes were on his feet and laced, Jett moved for the door.

He had the unfortunate habit of keeping in his phone in his left pants pocket, making it difficult to pull the phone out using only his right hand. Once freed, he used his thumb to call Shooter and get an update. He was moving fast, maneuvering around slower-moving patients and nurses along the way.

After meeting up with Shooter, who was still in the waiting room, they made their way to Shooter's car and headed back to Gulf Highway.

"We've got three patrols working the west end: DiCicco, Hancock, and DeeDee," Shooter said. "So far, nothing, no trace of the truck. We did find a body about a quarter mile down Gulf Highway, pretty badly mangled. We're not sure who it is but it looks like it might be one of the shooters."

"What about Robert? Any word? Anyone seen him?"

Shooter turned his reddened eyes towards Jett. "No. Nothing."

They drove down to Gulf Highway, turning west to follow the route of the truck. Shooter pointed out where the dead body was found as they drove. Yellow tape marked the area, and a part-time traffic officer stood by to prevent curious onlookers from messing with the scene before it had been more closely inspected by investigating officers. Jett waved a hand as they passed.

They passed the inlet to the lagoon on the west side of Mobile Road, then pulled over as one of the patrol cars approached from the other direction.

"Chief! Good to see you." It was Hancock.

"Thanks. Did you find anything?"

"No, sir. I canvassed between this here inlet bridge to the end of the lagoon. No sign of Robert or the truck."

"Damn it."

He just gotten similar reports from Daggett, known in the Department as DeeDee, and DiCicco. If the truck met up with someone, whether someone with a boat or another vehicle to move Robert, they would have found the abandoned truck. The places out on this end of the town were either condos with parking areas they had checked, or large, rental houses elevated above the ground making it easy to check for old trucks.

Where could they have gone?

"Keep looking, Hancock. We have to find Robert."

Hancock gave a wave of his hand and spun his car around to go back and cruise the area. Jett told Shooter to head back to where they found the body, and Shooter turned the cruiser around.

"Remember, you asked me to find out about that property on the waterway next to BODE, Inc.?" Shooter said as they drove back down Gulf Highway. "Turns out it's owned by a startup called White Sands Clean Energy. They're planning to build a solar farm on it, according to plans they filed with the state. Company's owned by an LLC out of Delaware named Energy Investors, but I can't find out anything about them."

"You checked the Delaware filings?"

"I did. It's owned by other LLCs, owned by other LLCs. I can't figure why it's legal to have all these dummy companies. Makes little things difficult, things like law enforcement and such."

They were passing an old two-story building that was once the Redwood Hotel but had been unused for the last ten years. After passing it, Jett turned his head suddenly to look back at the hulking dark brown building.

"Stop!" Shooter slammed the brakes and looked at Jett. "Go back—there's a workshop building at the back there."

Shooter turned to follow Jett's eyes, seeing the building behind the last empty business location on this side of White Sands.

"Shit." He cranked the wheel and hit the gas. The cruiser responded immediately and shot across the road. Shooter pulled into the lot and sped through it to the building at the back.

Shooter was out of the car, gun drawn, and reaching for the garage door handle by the time Jett managed to get out of the cruiser. Jett stepped to the other side of the door, signaling Shooter to stand ready as he pulled the door open. Shooter got into position, and Jett grabbed the door handle. With a firm pull, the door's rusted hinges squealed loudly as the door opened.

Shooter stared deep into the darkness inside.

"The truck," he said.

Jett looked in and then stepped inside the doorway. A door on the rear of the building was open, and Jett saw water rippling behind the building.

"Goddamnit. Go call it in, Shooter." He started into the building, looking over the truck as his eyes adjusted to the dim light. After a moment, he could easily see the holes in the truck where he'd shot it, and a large bloodstain on the front seat.

But no sign of Robert again.

He walked through to the back door and stepped down to the small dock where the boat had been tied up. He scanned the calm lagoon for signs of a boat passing recently. He saw a spot about 50 feet away where he once pulled a nice sized speckled trout out of the water, and to the west, the area where his own small dock and boat waited for him.

Shooter stepped through the doorway and looked around the lagoon.

"These guys are organized," Shooter said. "What are we up against here, Chief?"

"Damned if I know." He turned to the steps leading back to the garage. "But it's not good."

He boiled his choices down to two immediate actions: go back to the spot where the body was found or keep looking for Robert.

Investigation of the body might quickly yield helpful information: who he was, who he had associated with, where he worked, family and friends. That might be a good shortcut to finding Robert.

On the other hand, if he could somehow track Robert, he just might save the man's life.

Shooter waited quietly for Jett's next words.

"Shooter, get Daggett to pick up Melcott to investigate the scene where the body was found—we'll let the detectives do their work."

"OK. What're we doing?"

"We're going to get my boat and keep looking for Robert."

Shooter used his radio to get hold of DeeDee while Jett eased himself back into the car. He passed on the instructions, then drove Jett to his house on the edge of the .

They went to the boat at the back of Jett's house and as Jett started the boat's motor, Shooter untied the craft. They made a turn in the water and Jett began thinking about possible escape routes for someone. He knew there weren't roads going north to the Old Bay Road and travel back through town would be risky for the kidnappers.

Between the two options, it seemed most likely they met up somewhere close to the old hotel garage. Or somewhere along the north side of the lagoon.

Jett knew of several private docks there they could have gone, but someone would have heard or seen them docking and moving Robert. No one had reported anything unusual, so that didn't seem likely.

He was driving the boat towards the inlet when he remembered a spot he had used to meet up with friends back in high school. It was a small cove, hidden by reeds and grass, with a shallow approach.

And it was just a hundred feet off of the end of West Oyster Beach Drive, making it ideal for a quick change and escape.

He quickly turned the boat around and headed towards the area where he recalled the cove was located. He slowed as they approached the tall reeds obscuring the waterline. The reeds made it hard to tell where the little cove was, with stands growing out into the lagoon.

The shoreline had changed since Jett had last been in the area. He had trouble figuring out where the cove was.

"We're looking for a small inlet through those reeds," he told Shooter. "You gotta watch while we pass to be able to tell if there's a gap where an inlet is."

They made several false turns and stops before he finally recognized the gap where the water was just deep enough to let a boat slip through to a small landing.

Jett slowed the boat, the motor's propeller quieted to just low gurgling sounds in the water. He made a slow turn starboard to pass between two stands of reeds, then a slight turn to port as the boat rounded another outcropping of the plants.

As the boat cleared the outcropping, they saw the small boat grounded just out of the water.

Shooter jumped out of the boat as soon as he heard sand scratching the hull, into water up to his knees. He forcefully made his way to the waterline, then stepped up to the small craft. He looked in.

"He's not here."

"Check for tire tracks, footprints," Jett said. He grabbed the microphone for the radio in his boat and called for Hancock and any available officers to head immediately to West Oyster Beach Drive to continue the search for Robert as Shooter looked around the site.

"We're going to need some help here," Shooter said. "There's prints here, at least three men, two from the truck. Looks like one from the boat."

He looked up at Jett.

"Where the hell's Robert?"

Jett pulled out his cell phone and began scrolling through his contacts. He pressed a number, then put the phone to his ear.

"J.J.? It's Jett. I need all the help you can get me right away."

Jett filled County Prosecutor Joseph Jedediah Johnson on the status of the search, and current needs his department had to continue all the streams of investigation underway. Johnson promised to issue an emergency notice of a kidnapped officer across all of Southern Alabama. He also said he'd have sheriff's deputies and investigators from his office on the way to help any way Jett needed, including a contact he had in the Alabama State Investigation Bureau.

"I gotta get back to the office," Jett said after ending the call, looking at Shooter. "But I need you to stay here until the county guys arrive."

"Sure thing. I'll wait here and get a ride to my cruiser when I can get away."

Jett started dialing on his phone again.

"Thanks, Shooter," he said. His attention turned to his phone call. "Gwen—it's Jett. I need you to make some space in the conference room. We got a mess of people coming to help find Bobby."

21

The White Sands Police Headquarters conference room had been converted to a "war room" for only the second time in the department's history.

Just about six months ago the room was used to coordinate information on Joey Beaumont, a serial killer using empty condos on the beach to hide. During that investigation, Tana helped formulate a plan and catch the killer before outside investigators got involved.

But this time, the room was a beehive of law enforcement personnel including White Sands Police officers, Monroe County Sheriff's Deputies, and the county's Prosecutor's Office Special Investigations Detectives.

Information was beginning to be assembled, and Gwen was busily writing all of it on a whiteboard covering one wall.

So far, about all the investigation had determined was the name of the dead man found on Gulf Highway: Don Trahan, 27, no known address, no known relatives. Several officers who had served in Iraq recognized a tattoo on the man's right arm as one popular among employees of a private contractor hired to provide security for several bases.

He had died not from the gunshot wound received in his gunfight with Jett, but from head trauma caused by a vehicle. Investigators didn't quite understand how that had happened yet, but the injuries to his head, left arm, and neck were consistent.

The men stole the truck from an auto repair business in White Sands specializing in high performance vehicles sometime earlier in the night. Shooter had dusted the truck for fingerprints, but he only found partial prints in the box of the truck.

Jett, slumped in a desk chair in the middle of the room, was talking with Kris Linicum, the State Bureau of Investigation Major Crimes agent for the Mobile region. His phone buzzed with a call from Pat DiCicco.

"Chief, I just spoke to the Dauphin Island ferry driver, Roger Banks. He said he had three guys cross early this morning. From his descriptions, I don't think Robert was one them, but he said these guys were scary."

"What time was that? What's he mean by 'scary?'"

"He said it was his first run, so about 8:50 a.m. He noticed them when they got out of a black Suburban or GMC Yukon and stood at the railing."

"OK…"

"None of them said anything, they just kept looking around, nervous-like. He said they were all big, bulked up, dressed in the same black T-shirts and khaki pants."

"Did he notice where they went? Did he get a plate number?"

"No plate and no idea where they were going—but he did say it's most likely they were heading to Mobile. Maybe Mississippi."

"Good job, Pat. Got anything else?"

"No. I spoke to a couple who came over on the ferry, but they didn't remember the vehicle. Haven't found anyone else around this morning who witnessed anything."

"OK. Get yourself something to eat, then come in. We'll have a briefing sometime around 3 p.m. to get everyone current."

Jett looked at the whiteboard. One section had information on the truck and Trahan, another had details on the boat found on the lagoon.

A separate board had a timeline that Gwen had written:

0701: Robert calls Jett from Bougainville Shop and Go
0745: Unit 32-1 begins pursuit of truck on County Road 10
0748: Visual of truck lost on Mobile Road
0815: Truck spotted near Airport Road; Unit 32-1 in pursuit
0820: Two unidentified men fire upon Unit 32-1 on Mobile Road 300 feet south of Old Bay Road
0822: Shooters depart scene; turn west on Gulf Highway
0824: Units 32-2 and 32-8 in pursuit of shooters on Gulf Highway
0824: Body of D. Trahan (Shooter 2) found on Gulf Highway
1223: Truck used by shooters found at former Redwood Hotel garage on Gulf Highway

1255: Boat used by Shooter 1 located on lagoon below end of West 34th Street

Jett stretched his neck gingerly, trying to loosen the injured shoulder.

"Gwen—add this," he said, looking down at a notepad. The room suddenly became quiet as everyone waited to hear the updated information that Jett received.

"Add 'Suspects on ferry to Dauphin Island at 0850,'" he said. He looked at Kris and added, "That missing officer alert go as far as Pascagoula?"

She slowly shook her head. "I'll get it out immediately," she said.

Kris stood and went to the hallway to call her office and have the area alerted widened to include Southern Mississippi.

Jett fell back into the chair. He rubbed at his temples to ease the tension growing in his skull.

This whole matter was way out of control: kidnapping an officer, a shootout on Mobile Road, dead men on the side of Gulf Highway…Neither the county prosecutor nor he would be able to hold off the press much longer. Things could only get worse after that.

On top of that, he had to find Robert—and find him fast. These guys were deadly, serious, and well-organized.

Kris came back into the room and Jett called out to her.

"Kris, what do you make of this?" he asked her when she pulled up an office chair to sit next to him. "I can't figure what to make of people who would kidnap an officer, shoot at a police car on a major roadway…and for what?"

"Have your officers had any unusual interactions lately?" she asked. She watched Jett's expression closely as she spoke. "Any suspicious characters seen in town, or anything like that?"

"No. It's off season and the town has been really quiet." He nervously tapped the back of his left hand with a pencil.

"Nothing out of the ordinary?"

Jett sat up. "Bobby said something about a barge on the Intracoastal Waterway the other night. He said it stopped at a spot where there's no dock and appeared to loading or unloading something."

"What was the cargo?"

"He couldn't tell. He tried to get close to find out, but it started backtracking as soon as he got close and…"

Jett turned to face Kris.

"He said he thought he heard voices, some like people issuing orders and young women. Do you think this could involve the barge Robert saw on the Intracoastal?"

Kris straightened her black suit jacket and wiggled back in the chair. She pushed her red hair sweeping across her forehead back around an ear and sighed.

"There's a few possibilities here, Chief," she said. "What exactly you got, I don't know but it sounds like your man may have some across some kind of trafficking operation. Between the state and the feds, there are a lot of ongoing investigations along the coast…drug trafficking, human trafficking, stolen goods…hell, you name it."

She said she knew of a few specific investigations in the Gulf—there was a lot of drug and human trafficking activity from Houston to Tampa. The human trafficking involved mostly Asian victims coming in from Korea and China, but also Latinas. She added there were a couple of undercover things happening closer to White Sands between Biloxi and Pensacola.

"I don't know the specifics," she said. "I called a friend at ICE, see if he knew anything. He only said Homeland Security has been pretty busy lately breaking up operators out of Uzbekistan, and they can be pretty rough characters."

"This ain't them," Jett said. "These are homegrown guys…at least, they seem to be."

"Well, don't be too sure. These guys recruit from around the world, including the good ol' US of A. Lot of people willing to do bad things, if the pay is right."

She took a drink from her water bottle and studied the timeline on the board.

"But if that's what it is, what we don't know is which way they're trafficking. It seems unusual."

"How so?"

"First, most of them try to offload their…let's call it 'cargo'…somewhere offshore, breaking it down into smaller shipments to bring ashore. Easier to avoid detection and move about that way. But where would they be dropping off a shipment—even a small one— here? Kinda hard to hide more than a handful of people or relatively small quantity of drugs or stolen goods in such a small town, yet they used a very large vessel to bring it in."

She paused for another drink.

"On the other hand, if they're picking up, then the same question kinda arises: how did the cargo get here without drawing attention?"

She paused, thinking through the questions in her mind.

"And then there's the violence," she added. "We got us some real bad guys here."

"That's putting it mildly."

Jett turned and reached for his cup of coffee on a desk behind him. He sipped it, made a face.

"No good?" Kris asked, a small grin on her face.

"Cold. Drinking it anyway."

As if to prove it, he raised the cup and took a deep drink, taking in half the contents, before putting it back on the desk. He rubbed his shoulder, trying to loosen muscles tightened from the fresh wound.

"So, where do we go from here?"

"We've got the all-points out for your man. We've got the Coast Guard checking barges in the area, but there are a lot of them and as you know, this part of the Gulf has lots of hiding places."

Jett knew that was true. Two hundred years ago, the area was a favorite hiding spot for pirates. No less than Jean LaFitte, perhaps the most famous pirate—or privateer, depending on your viewpoint and perhaps the year—is rumored to have hidden treasure in the many bays along the Gulf Coast from Louisiana to Florida. LaFitte often stopped at Dauphin Island to unload stolen cargo, or carry stolen slaves up to Mobile, even as far back as when Mobile was Spanish territory.

"We don't have the name of the barge; we don't have a very definite description of the craft," Kris continued. "We don't have any description of the men who kidnapped Robert, and we don't know where they are headed."

"That pretty well sums it up." Jett put his head in his hands. He was tired, hungry, and he hadn't shaved, showered or eaten since he jumped out of bed to pick up Robert in Bougainville almost eight hours earlier.

It was all catching up, but he couldn't risk missing an important bit of information or, with luck, a report that someone found Robert.

After all, they're sure to let him go, Jett thought. They might rough him up a bit—that's OK, Robert could take it.

But no one would be crazy enough to cause him any serious harm.

"This job used to be so much easier," Jett said. His head hung down, and stared into his coffee cup, deep in thought. "I never thought I'd see shit like this go down in White Sands."

Kris watched him carefully, trying to find the right words. What do you tell someone the first time they wake up in a real-life nightmare?

Tell him the world's changing? That the bad guys are getting tougher and better equipped than law enforcement can keep up with?

"I remember Dad telling me just before he put his badge down, that it was going to get worse." He took a deep drink and turned towards Kris. "I sure as hell didn't know what he was talking about. If I had, I wouldn't have taken on the job. I'm not equipped for it."

"Jett, we all find ourselves in shit at some time or another. I've been there, too…that moment you ask yourself how you got in a position where your life is up for grabs and you're not sure why you're doing it."

Kris waited before continuing, giving Jett a chance to let what she'd said sink in.

"But then you think about who you're protecting, who you're doing it for—your family, your friends. Your community. Then it gets clearer."

Jett looked at her. He was about to say something about how he doesn't have any family anymore. How his only "friend" is a messed-up emigre from Missouri who is so screwed up, it's impossible to talk to her. Everyone else he knows is an employee or another resident of the town demanding he "take care" of something.

"I'm just not the right guy here, Kris," he said. "I'm not doing this because of a drive to save the world. I'm only here because my father was chief, and when he left, no one else would do it."

Kris could see he knew that wasn't entirely true, but she let it alone.

"You will find your man, and you will find these bastards, and you will save the lives of many people. Don't ever forget that, Jett."

He rubbed his temples. His slackened face showed his exhaustion.

"Yeah. We'll get 'em." Jett's voice was drained of emotion.

Less than half an hour after the missing officer alert went out to parts of Western Florida and Eastern Mississippi, Gwen received a call.

She listened carefully, jotting notes on a pad, then hung up the phone. She tore the page off the pad, the slowly stood, pushing the chair back with her legs. She started walking towards Jett, with her eyes fixed on him across the room. She stopped in front of Jett.

"Jett, we got a call about Robert," she said. "They think they found him in Pascagoula."

Jett studied her face.

"Alive?"

Gwen just held out the slip of paper for Jett.

22

Jett pulled into Pascagoula on U.S. 90. It was nearing sunset, and the growing dark matched his mood. There was pounding in his head and his right hand was shaking. The uncontrollable motion started as soon as he pulled off the ferry at Dauphin Island, getting more and more violent as he drew nearer to Pascagoula in his Explorer.

The radio was blasting Metallica—he hoped the loud music and pounding guitars would chase the thoughts of what lie ahead out of his head, but it wasn't succeeding. Hetfield's throaty vocals were uncharacteristically weak and only served to give Jett a headache.

It took three tries for his shaking finger to hit the radio's scan button, and it landed on a gospel station. Not helpful; another scan. Another gospel channel. Scan again and Brad Paisley was singing "Another American Saturday Night," which Jett normally enjoyed but was completely out of place in his head today, so he scanned again. And again. And again.

Two rap stations, one R&B and four more gospel channels, and he was back to Metallica. Give it up.

He sat back.

"We're off to Never… Neverland…We're off to…"

Jett shut the radio off.

He wished Tana was with him. He wished he hadn't pushed her away. Why was it such a problem for him when she was around?

His mind drifted back to a Sunday afternoon just eight weeks ago. The two of them were drifting in his boat on the lagoon. He watched Tana sitting peacefully and still, holding a fishing line in the water. The curve of her cheek and chin line fascinated him; so delicate, yet she was so strong.

"Jesus, you never tire of fishing," he said.

Tana turned towards him. He loved how the light reflected off the lake illuminated her hair and flashed in her eyes. He wanted to take her in his arms.

"It's the only activity I know that lets me shut out everything and be still."

It was such a peaceful moment. It seemed like the right time to ask her, but he let it pass.

Highway 90 turned into Denny Avenue, and Jett followed it to the exit at Pascagoula Street. A left to turn onto Live Oak Boulevard brought him to the police department headquarters.

Jett wiped beads of sweat growing on his forehead as he pulled into the department's parking lot. After parking in the first row, he carefully twisted his body so he could open the door with his right hand. He grimaced as a bolt of pain from his shoulder shot through his body.

He took a breath, then snapped the door open and stepped out of the White Sands Police car he'd taken, his knees buckling slightly as he put his weight down. Before closing the door, he stood and waited for a flush of dizziness to pass.

He made his way to the entrance of the department. He took a deep breath before pulling the door open, then walked in. He stopped at the window in the waiting room and a sergeant stood and approached.

"I have a meeting with Chief Mark. My name is Jett Jeanrette."

"One moment. You can have a seat right there." The sergeant pointed to a bench next to a trophy case behind Jett.

Jett turned and looked. "Thank you."

He slumped onto the bench, trying to hide his shaking right hand under the sling. Nervously, his leg twitched and tapped.

A few minutes later a door next to the bench opened, and a heavy-set Black man in a dark blue Pascagoula Police uniform stood before him.

"Chief Jeanrette, Sam Mark. I'm sorry we meet this way." He extended a thick hand towards Jett, and when Jett stood to grasp it, gave Jett a firm shake.

"Chief Mark. Thank you." Jett was a full head taller than the chief, but what the Mississippi man lacked in height he made up for in solid bulk.

"Come in. Please, friends just call me Mark." He stepped aside to hold the door open for Jett.

They walked down to the chief's office, where Jett sat in a chair in front of Mark's cluttered desk. Mark picked up his phone and spoke into it after a moment. "Claire, would you please call the coroner's office and tell them Chief Jeanrette from White Sands is here? Then get a reservation at the steakhouse for later."

He put the phone down and looked at Jett. His intense eyes were studying Jett, and he swallowed before speaking.

"I never had to do what I'm asking you to do, and I can't imagine what you must be going through."

Jett looked down. He was still trying to hide his shaking hand. "I appreciate that, Chief...er, Mark. Thank you."

Mark bent down to open a drawer in his desk. He pulled out a bottle of rye and two glasses.

"I reckon we best get over to the coroner's office and get this done," he said while pouring a couple of fingers of whiskey into the glasses. "But first."

He lifted one glass to Jett.

Jett took the glass and drained it. He put it down on the chief's desk and noticed Mark was holding an envelope in his other hand. Mark studied Jett's face as he gently placed the envelope in front of Jett.

"This here is all we found on him."

Jett gingerly picked up the envelope. It was light. The sound of small pieces of metal, keys or coins maybe, tinkled in the envelope as Jett lifted it up.

"Thank you." Mark watched the shaking hand holding the envelope, then stood and said, "Come on."

When Jett stood and turned to leave the office, Mark gently placed a hand on his shoulder. He guided Jett towards a door that lead to the rear parking lot.

"How long you been chief there in White Sands?" Mark asked quietly as they walked towards his car.

"I took over after my dad died in 2008." Jett was looking at the envelope, unsure if he wanted to open it.

"My kids like to visit White Sands," Mark said. "Wife's folks have a condo on the beach, and we go once or twice a year for a week. Just get away, you know."

They reached the car and climbed in at the same time.

Mark started the car and began backing out. "Nice place. You got a nice town there."

Jett sat straight, staring blankly out the windshield. He struggled to think of a response, but his mind was a vacuum.

They drove on in silence. The coroner's office was only a couple of miles away. Before Jett realized it, they were parking outside the office. Mark again carefully guided Jett into the building, and they were met by a young woman standing in an open doorway down the hall.

"Chief Mark, it's good to see you," she said. As deputy medical examiner, Joyce Demit conducted many of the investigatory examinations for what Mississippi calls "deaths affecting the public interest." She worked alongside the police department, often giving Mark or one of his captains the results and conclusions of the department's investigations.

"You must be Chief Jeanrette," she said, looking at Jett while extending her hand. "Joyce Demit. Please follow me."

The three of them stepped into a room with a large curtained window. They lined up, Demit and Mark on either side of Jett. Mark again put his hand on Jett's shoulder.

"Now, I'm going to open this curtain in a minute. You know how this goes. I only need you to ID him. Don't be worrying about anything else right now, Jett."

Jett took a deep breath.

"You set?" Jett nodded.

Mark knocked on the glass, then after a moment pulled a cord to open the curtains.

Robert's body lay on a steel table, covered with a thin sheet. An orderly lifted the sheet, revealing a face that Jett couldn't place at first. He knew it was someone he knew, but…

Jett turned away. "Fuck."

"That your man, Robert Gulliford?"

Jett turned to Mark. He looked the chief up and down, trying to regain his composure.

"Yes. That's him. I think so."

"Alright. We're done here."

The two police chiefs stepped back into the hallway and headed towards the exit.

"God damn it," Mark grumbled. "I was truly hoping it wouldn't be. I'm sorry, Jett."

They walked towards the car in silence.

"Was he a good cop?"

"Yeah, he was. Good man, good cop."

They got in the car, and Mark started the engine.

"I was kind of hoping to promote him soon," Jett said. "He's got a wife and little boy. Had his head on straight. Good man. Think he could have made chief himself."

"You got any idea of what's going on here?"

Jett told Mark about Robert's first disappearance, the search for him, and the shootout. In the corner of his eye, he could see Mark's astonished face as he told the story.

"Dear Lord. This all happened in White Sands? Today?"

"Yes. Well, White Sands and Bougainville."

"Who you think is behind it? How can I help?" Mark was pulling onto Highway 90 and heading west. The road became a bridge and rose over the Pascagoula River. Jett watched the river pass by, then an industrial area with riverside warehouses, and another stretch of businesses.

"I really don't know what to do, Mark. I can't believe what's going on. We got some people down from Mobile and Montgomery, but this is new territory for us. For me."

Mark pulled off the highway onto a street, then pulled to the curb. He turned towards Jett.

"If I go up this way about a mile, there's a good place where we can get dinner and a couple of drinks." He pointed to an intersection just ahead of them.

"I take a right there, and I can show you where we found Robert's body."

He waited a minute.

"If you want."

Jett looked down the road. It headed back towards the river, back towards the industrial area.

"Yes," he said. "Show me."

"Alright, then." Mark hit the gas and pulled onto the road, took the right turn and headed to the pull-off at the river that lead to the spot where they'd discovered Robert's body. As they neared the spot, he began detailing what led to the body being found.

"We received a report early this morning from a fishing boat that a body was on the shore about a quarter-mile down from Riverside Road—that's this road we're on. Two officers came down, then the coroner's office responded to retrieve the body. Course, we didn't know who it was—but when I saw your alert from Mobile, I figured we should contact you."

"Thank you for that, Mark."

"We got to help each other—that's the best help a cop can get."

"Uh-huh." Jett nodded. He was leaning forward, looking at the river bank and side of the road through the car's windshield.

Mark stopped the car and stepped out. As soon as he'd turned off the engine, Jett had his door open and was ready to jump out. They stepped to the front of the car, then Mark started walking towards the river.

After climbing down the side of a small rise, they stood on low-lying land. The ground was soft, and small pools of water were visible through the low vegetation growing between them and the river.

"This area ahead of us is a marsh, starting about 20 feet out," Mark said. "I wouldn't go any further on foot."

He raised an arm and pointed toward the Pascagoula High Rise Bridge. "About 50 feet in front of us in that direction there's a little clearing. That's where his body was."

Mark studied Jett's face as he said this, unsure of what his reaction would be.

"Near as we can figure at this point, he died somewhere else and was brought here."

"You haven't done an autopsy yet—how can you tell that?"

"It looks like he drowned. There's no other indication of a possible cause of death, no cuts, deep bruising, gun wounds. But when we brought him in, his lungs were full of water. Ms. Demit was smart enough to collect and analyze some of the water he expelled. She tells me it was fresh water, not salinity like he'd have if he drowned here."

Jett thought about this. "Could he have drowned upstream, further from the Gulf?"

"Yes, but here's the thing—the water in his lungs had chlorine in it. He drowned in tap water. What it looks like, anyway. We'll know more after the autopsy, but I think Ms. Demit is on target."

"So…" Jett was trying to wrap his head around this. How could he drown in tap water? "How…what did they do?"

"That's one theory." Mark took a breath. "After what you told me about what all happened, I gotta ask: you think he could have been waterboarded? Seems like the kind of people who'd do that."

Jett felt the ground shifting under his feet. What kind of people were they dealing with? Shootouts with the police? Kidnapping police officers? Waterboarding a cop? The descriptions were ex-military, but what are they doing that would require such extreme actions?

"I'm sorry. That just doesn't make sense to me. Who would do this?

I know we've got some mean mothers running around, but what the hell are they doing they would kidnap and drown a cop?"

Mark stepped carefully back towards the car.

"I don't know, but it ain't good."

Jett and Mark returned to the car in silence. Jett was unsteady as he slowly walked to the car, his face contorted in confusion. He reached out and rested on the hood of the car.

"I can't...I don't..." He gave Mark a pleading look. "I just don't know where to go from here."

"We'll get them," Mark reassured him. "It won't be pretty when we do, but we will. Have you eaten today?"

23

Leaves and branches and bits of debris drifted on the Intracoastal Waterway, slowly moving eastward towards Perdido. Tana, sitting on a picnic bench and watching, finding the slow motion and setting sun soothing.

This is where Robert sat as the barge had passed by two days ago. Tana watched a tree branch drifting in the water, following its drift down the canal. She followed the drifting wood until it was a few hundred feet away, nearly out of sight.

The events of the past two days were clouding her head. She'd found it impossible to focus on anything in the afternoon, except for her ideas about checking out the barge with cameras. She'd almost struck an elderly woman walking along the roadside on Intracoastal Boulevard, she was so distracted as she drove.

That's why she pulled over and came to the picnic table. Sit here, watching things drift by let her unchain the images in her head, balaclavas, and images of the shootout, Robert's wife glaring at Jett, and the video of men following Robert.

The sound of an approaching boat broke the quiet and Tana turned to watch the craft slowly motoring on the canal. As it grew closer, she could see it wasn't a barge like Robert had described to her, but more like a fishing boat, maybe a shrimp boat.

She watched the chubby vessel move past, and thought about the man she saw just a little further down the waterway from where she was sitting, the man called Spence who told her about a barge stopping there.

It all made some sense if someone was using the waterway to illegally move something, stolen goods or drugs seemed likely. Spence

119

said something about a plane and a bus, also.

So, someone flew goods or drugs to White Sands, then put them on the barge to take them…where? Tana thought. Or did they bring the illicit goods on the barge, then flew it out?

Flying illicit things into the Gulf Coast wasn't a new idea. There had been pilots in the '80s and '90s flying drugs for Colombian cartels; they went to the Florida coast. Tana wasn't sure where the planes started from, she didn't think they could make it all the way to White Sands, but she didn't know.

And, of course, the area did have an extensive history of stolen goods being moved through the area on boats—Tana recalled a speaker she'd seen at the White Sands museum discussing the exploits of Jean Lafitte and Gasparillo in the area. The lakes and bays between Mobile Bay and Pensacola provided lots of ideal spots for hiding stolen goods, people, and even ships.

So it seems Robert saw something he shouldn't have, a shipment of stolen goods or drugs being transferred. And this made some sense, Tana thought, because of White Sands' location away from major cities and transportation hubs—sort of an "out-of-sight" situation.

Plus the coming and going of tourists, who often make up the vast majority of people here, means such movements rarely get noticed.

But Robert noticed. He noticed, and he acted, and in response, some very bad people are reacting.

Guys who would snatch a police officer, or stage a shoot out in broad daylight, seem like members of a drug-smuggling ring, people living in a very lucrative, very violent world.

Part of Tana wanted to call Jett, to talk about the barge and Robert, to talk about his injuries, to see how he was.

Maybe to open the door to try again. Maybe talk about how she can't let herself get close to him…

A little voice in her head told her to stay clear, not just of Jett, but also not to get any more involved in whatever is going on. Jett and the state investigators—and probably the DEA before the end of the day—can handle it. That's their job, and more power to them.

She drove halfway to Mobile earlier, planning to purchase cameras she could attach to trees in the area where Robert had seen the barge stop. But she turned around and came back to White Sands, uncertain whether she wanted to get further involved. That was the first thing the little voice told her she listened to.

And the voice told Tana to let Jett call her when he wants to talk, that he'll probably only call when he needs to be bailed out of some situation, again…

She had promised to finish studying the robberies and report back to the Sheriff's Office in the morning. She still hadn't found answers to her questions. The robbers' actions seemed off a bit and didn't add up. It was almost like they weren't after the money at all, she thought.

No matter how much she tried, she couldn't find a way to make sense of this—or forget about the barge. There was too much going on. She needed to stay clear of Jett, and investigations, and everything for a while.

With that, Tana stood and walked to her Jeep. The last light of the sun kept the sky bright, but soon it would be dark. Tana decided dinner at a sushi bar next to the movie theater on Mobile Road was what she needed.

She took the bypass road that cut north to Airport Road, then back towards Mobile Road and the strip mall with her favorite restaurant.

A few minutes later and she was driving past the edge of the airport property, watching a small Cessna landing on a runway running parallel to the road. The plane bobbed once on the tarmac, then settled on the ground and taxied its way towards the small building that served as the airport terminal.

Tana watched the plane rolling along. It neared the terminal and past an area crowded with small planes in front of a hangar. Next to the hangar was a larger building that served as a hangar for BODE, Inc.

A massive cargo plane was parked in front of the big hangar, a huge "B" on the tail.

What was it Spence said about a plane landing ahead of the barge?

24

Tana ate without tasting her food, absent-mindedly feeding herself while her mind wandered through random thoughts about Bobby, barges and balaclavas. She paid for her meal and left without saying a word to the restaurant staff, and climbed into the Jeep in a daze.

Her head again filled with images and thoughts she couldn't sort, couldn't order. They didn't make sense to her, flashing in her mind then disappearing before she had a chance to consider them. Men dashing into a convenience store...Jett getting shot...Bobby offering a beignet...John Stone lying dead...the blue and gold Sheriff's Department logo...an unknown figure suddenly dropping to the ground...accommodation barges...

In her distracted state, she drove back to Airport Road, instead of just turning down Mobile Road in a more direct route to her home. It was late, and the road was dark—even the lights at the airport were dimmed as if it was closed.

The huge plane she'd noticed earlier was not sitting next to the hangar. It was rolling toward the runway in the dark.

Tana slowed to watch the plane make its way to the runway. The plane was unusual, its fat body had overhead wings, and wheels jutted from the bottom of the two turbo-prop engines. The BODE "B" insignia emblazoned on the tail was barely visible in low light.

As Tana watched, the plane began rolling faster, gaining speed for take-off. At the same time, she heard the roar of the powerful engines, and soon, the plane was lifting off the ground near the end of the runway.

Tana watched the plane rise into the night sky, the diminishing lights vanishing among the night's stars.

Tana realized she was driving slowly, distracted by the plane's take-off. Lights brightened her rear-view mirror, and she sped up towards the bypass.

At the corner, she turned to backtrack the route she'd followed on the way to the restaurant, and the two vehicles she'd been holding up on Airport Road followed.

Soon, they were close behind her again, so she sped up.

But instead of putting distance between herself and the vehicle behind her, it pulled into the other lane and accelerated to pass her.

Once in front, the vehicle slowed until Tana had to brake just as the second vehicle behind her pulled up within inches of her rear bumper. Soon, she was at a dead stop between two large SUVs.

As she watched in her outside mirror, a man exited the vehicle behind her and walked to the passenger side of her Jeep. He opened in and climbed in without saying a word.

"We need you to follow the directions I give you without any trouble."

Tana studied the man. He was young, fit, and wore a polo shirt with "BODE, Inc." embroidered on the chest. He was also armed.

Tana looked at her mirror again and saw another man had exited the SUV behind her and one from the vehicle in front. Both men held guns. She turned to the man beside her.

"Where to?"

The man signaled, and after the others returned to their vehicles, he told her to follow the vehicle in front. The vehicle pulled out, and Tana followed with the third vehicle still right behind her.

The caravan turned on BODE Drive. Tana followed the lead vehicle onto the BODE property. They passed the guardhouse without stopping and turned to park at an office building near the front of the property.

As soon as she stopped, she hopped out of her Jeep and stood with her arms crossed.

"What the hell is this?" she demanded of the men climbing out of the SUV parked next to her Jeep.

One man reached to grab her elbow, and she swung away from him.

"I'll follow, but don't touch me." She glared at him, and the man momentarily froze.

"Seth, stop. It's OK, Miss. Please, come with me." The leader of the group had been the one to climb into Tana's Jeep, and he stood on the sidewalk in front of the offices. He waved Tana forward and turned to walk to the doors.

Tana followed the man into the building, while Seth and the others kept pace behind. The building was dark, except for light from an office ahead. The office had a small, circular table with four chairs around it, and pictures of oil wells, rigs, derricks, pipes, and trucks lining the panelled walls.

"Have a seat. Mr. Basko will be right in." He stood for a moment, looking at Tana. "Can I get you something to drink?"

Tana looked at him. "Are you serious?"

He snorted, then turned and walked out, closing the door behind him.

About a minute later, he opened the door and stepped in, followed by a short, rotund man with a ruddy face. He wore golf attire, shirt and pants, as if he'd just finished 18 holes and parked the cart even though it was well past sunset.

"OK, then," he said, dropping into one of the chairs. "Who are you?"

"Who am I? I'm the person your security goons kidnapped. Who are you?"

The man sat back and chuckled. "I appreciate that, I surely do. I'm Sandy Basko."

He stuck his hand out for Tana to shake, but withdrew it when it was clear she would not reciprocate.

Tana studied the legendary billionaire. He was famous for having consolidated oil services by buying up struggling independents during downturns. The size of his acquisitions grew, and he was now sitting atop an empire competing with Halliburton.

His company was based in Houston, but it wasn't a secret his office was in White Sands, somewhere in the huge facility he'd built in the '90s.

"What do you want, Mr. Basko?" Tana kept her eyes on him, gauging his reactions.

"Well, now, Missy, I tell you what," he said. He was looking at his hands while wiping his palms across each other, as if there was a speck of dirt on one. "What I *want* is to understand why you're so interested in my property."

"What?"

"Come on now, Missy, I know…"

"My name is Montana Stone."

"Ah, Miss Stone. As I was saying, I know you've been trespassing on my property—I heard about your encounter with my security the other day down by the canal." He turned and gave Seth a look that Tana knew meant he had been there when she was confronted—he was the one she thought of as 'Quiet Man.'

"I see. Well, your man here told me it was private property, so I left. Can I go now?"

Basko sighed.

"Not so fast, Miss Stone. Why you back here tonight?"

Basko's question confused Tana. She hadn't been back to the campsite or picnic area or whatever the hell the clearing by the waterway was. What did he mean "back here?"

"Mr. Basko," Tana leaned forward. "I don't know what you've been told, but I haven't been back anywhere on your property. I'm sorry you're misinformed, but I think I'll exercise my right to leave now."

She stood, but Basko signaled her to sit back down.

"If you don't mind, Miss Stone. I didn't mean exactly that." He turned to Quiet Man and waved him to leave the room. "Close the door, too."

Basko studied Tana's face. "You a pretty tough gal, ain't ya? And so pretty. How did you come to be that way?"

"Pretty or tough?"

Basko slapped the table and laughed, then looked at her. "Are you from Texas? You sure seem like a Texas gal."

"I'm from Missouri, you know, the 'Show Me State,' as in, 'show me the way out.'"

Basko kept chuckling.

"Miss Stone, I've been having some trouble lately with people spying on my operations. Competitors and such. I've had to increase security here and taken some unusual steps."

He stood and stretched, then tried to stifle a yawn. He bent and rested his arms on the back of the chair he'd been sitting in.

"I've asked my guys to keep an eye out for people coming by at odd times or multiple times, and things like that. They…" He jerked his head towards the door to indicate his security team. "They tell me they saw you watching Anton take off, so I wanted to talk to you."

"Anton? Who the hell is Anton?"

"Oh, that's what I call my plane, big ol' Russian cargo plane. Took off about 15 minutes ago now."

He paused.

"It's an Antonov AN-26, so I call it 'Anton.' Bit easier to say and less commie-like."

"I wasn't 'watching,' I was driving on Airport Road. Big

difference."

"Says you." Basko's demeanor suddenly changed. "I don't know who you are or what you might be up to, but don't let my dogs catch you around here again. My head of security is a bit of a fanatic about protecting my company and me, and I can't always be here to make sure he doesn't get carried away."

He reached out for the door handle. "Like I say, we've been having a bit of trouble with industrial spying lately."

He looked Tana up and down lecherously.

"And you look like a 'honeypot' to me."

He opened the door and walked out of the room.

Tana didn't understand the "honeypot" reference, and didn't understand why Basko found it so important to talk to her.

She figured it must be related to the day she dropped the guard who had accosted her previously; maybe her response had been taken as a sign of her being some kind of an industrial spy.

She slowly stood and started for the door. Just as she stepped through, Quiet Man stepped in front of her.

"Real quick, before you go…" He stepped aside for Tana to pass, and started walking alongside her as she headed for the door. "Don't come around here again. Don't drive on Airport Road, don't go to the canal. Just stay away."

Tana looked at him. He wasn't speaking threateningly, and his words almost sounded as if he was genuinely concerned.

As she walked through the door, he grabbed her arm.

"Basko's not shitting about his head of security. The man's dangerous."

Tana studied his face. He wasn't lying. She went to the Jeep, opened the door, then took another look at Quiet Man. He was standing with the office door open, watching her.

She was surprised when he waved before turning around and going back into the dark of the empty offices.

25

Tana drove through the gates at the front of the BODE property. Two security guards stood outside the guardhouse, watching her pull onto BODE Drive.

Something about the men seemed familiar to Tana. It wasn't until just before she pulled into the driveway at her house that she remembered why: they were two of the men who walked in—then out––at Pixie's, just after Robert left. Now she knew all three worked for Basko.

She mulled this over while climbing out of her Jeep. Lost in thought, she didn't notice the two shadows that stepped up behind her and pulled a black hood over her head. Someone pulled her arms behind her back, and quickly tied them with a plastic tie.

Tana was completely disoriented for a moment, then began screaming. The men picked her up, and carried her before carelessly tossing her into the back of a vehicle.

"Alright, let's go," Tana heard one of the men say.

"Not yet." She felt hands grab her legs. Something was quickly wrapped around her ankles, shackling her even more. Tana tried to kick, but it felt feeble and useless to do so with her ankles held together.

The hands released her legs. As she squirmed trying to get free, hands grabbed her hips. One hand pressed hard on her stomach, holding her down. The other hand searched, feeling her butt and between her legs.

"No!" Tana kicks with her legs, but she kicked air.

The hand moved around her thighs.

"No. No," she yelled, panicked.

"Stop it," a voice said.

"Fuck you. She's not going anywhere."

A hand grasped her breast.

"You fucking pig." Tana tried to fight back, but her movements were too limited to be threatening. She braced for what would come next.

"I said stop." Suddenly, there was scuffling. The two men were fighting, but Tana couldn't tell what was happening. The fighting stopped, and she heard the men breathing deeply after their battle.

"What the fuck do you care? She's gonna get it sooner or later, asshole."

"Mironoff said to bring her in. That doesn't mean rape her."

"You're such a pussy." Tana heard more scuffling and the dull thud of a punch, followed by a low grunt. A body slumped against the vehicle, then to the ground. Then silence.

The rear gate of the vehicle closed.

"Get your fucking ass up and in the truck now, or I'll leave you here." There was more said, but muffled through the glass as the men walked to the front of the vehicle and got in.

They drove in silence. Tana felt the vehicle moving and turning, stopping and starting on its way somewhere.

After almost half an hour, the vehicle stopped. The men got out and walked back to open the rear door.

"You got it ready?" Tana could tell the man who had touched her said this. Even under the hood, she felt his eyes lasciviously on her.

They rolled onto her side. She fought against their pushing and holding, but they held her firmly. She felt a sharp pain in her arm, and within seconds, a numbing spread through her body. Another couple of seconds and she went limp.

Sometime later, conversation between the two men wedged its way into her head. She was still disoriented, drifting in the dark under the hood and under the influence of some drug.

She felt a bobbing motion and heard a steady humming sound and water slapping the other side of whatever her head was resting on.

As her head cleared, she tried speaking. Her tongue was heavy and uncooperative. She wanted to ask if she was on the barge, but it came out as "Shish the barj?"

The motor slowed, then stopped. The boat struck something hard, and Tana's head bumped against the side of the boat. She was still numb and foggy, and while it didn't hurt when her head hit the side of the boat, she sensed she would feel it later.

The boat jostled as the men moved about. They pulled her up, then slipped a rope around her body, under her arms. She felt the creep's hand grab her breast again, and wished she could know who he was so she could make sure to pay him back later.

The rope pulled and lifted Tana upwards and onto a platform of some kind. Still fighting the drug's effects, she couldn't fix where she was but had a sense she was on a larger boat. Maybe it was Robert's barge.

Men's voices approached and then stopped.

"This is the woman?" A deep voice asked. Even in the few words spoken, Tana sensed the speaker's coldness. There was an accent in the way some words came out, but she couldn't place it. "This is woman Basko thinks is spying on him?"

"Yes, sir."

Tana felt a presence move close to her. Two men were holding her, her legs too uncontrolled to hold her up.

"Ung…" Tana tried to speak again, but her tongue wouldn't move.

She sensed the presence in front of her was studying her somehow. "Wha're you wan?"

"Don't you worry, little precious. We take good care of you."

There was some chattering between the men, but Tana couldn't follow it. Someone cut the ties holding her arms and ankles. She tried to move them, but found them unresponsive, as much due to having been tied for so long as from the drug they'd given her.

Someone pulled the hood off her face at the same time she felt another sting in her arm.

Her eyes blurred, but she saw the shadow of an enormously large man in front of her. She couldn't make out any features of his face, but could see he was bald, or nearly so, with a wide face and small eyes.

She felt the world start to go droopy again.

"She's cute."

It was getting cloudier.

"Yes, we can…"

The black took over, and Tana passed out.

She sensed movement and lights and forced her eyes to open. The men were carrying her down a hallway. They stopped to open a door, and before Tana could figure out where she was, she blacked out again.

She woke sometime later as the men opened a door to a dark room and took her inside. They let her slide to the floor, then turned to leave.

"Got…to…" Tana tried to concentrate on opening her eyes.

She was able to force her eyes open enough to see several other women around her in the room. The seemed young, Latina, and stoned, Tana thought. Just like me.

She tried to understand what was happening, but her mind was too clouded by drugs. Maybe it's heroin, she thought.

She drifted again, and in the dark of the little room, the feeling was overwhelming. She felt warm and relaxed, as if a heavy blanket had been pulled over her.

The room faded into black, and Tana passed out again.

26

Tana was flying. Well, not flying yet, just taking off, gaining elevation like a bird climbing higher into the sky. She felt weightless, gliding through air over a beach and water.

"Stand up." A voice commanded, interrupting her flight.

"Can you stand up?" Tana struggled to open her eyes. A man stood in front of her, trying to hold her upright in a standing position. He was taller than she, so he crouched a bit to hold her. He looked familiar somehow.

"I…ugh…a bird…" Tana's words still came out as gibberish.

He lightly tapped her face.

"Hey, come on. You need to wake up."

He pulled a tube like a cigar tube out of a pocket, and used his mouth to pull a cap off one end. She watched his hand with the tube move down to her arm and jab the tube at her shoulder.

Another sharp pain.

"Ow…" Tana was still limp, but the man kept a tight hold on her to keep her from falling.

A second later, a powerful energy rushed through her veins. It started in her arms and legs, and moved up through her body.

The room seemed to get brighter, and she realized she was moving again. The man was carrying her down a hallway.

"C'mon. Wake up."

"Whad…you…do? Feels…great."

"Good. Get yourself ready."

Tana recognized his voice—he was one of the men at BODE, when she spoke to Basko.

"Hey! Are you…" Her words formed more clearly now, but the

words she wanted to say disappeared before she could say them.

"Quiet!"

"Yes! Quiet Man, you're Quiet Man. I'm glad you're not Mr. Grabby Hands."

She tried to stop her feet from dragging on the floor.

"You're..my..." What was the word she wanted to say? She tried to drift back into the cloud to find the word, but found she couldn't. A nervous energy was building in her body, filling her arms and legs, and pushing away the clouds in her head.

"...Hero?"

He guided her through a door. They were outside now, on a narrow walkway on the side of a boat. She peered over the edge of the boat.

"This a barge?" She was still wobbly, but could almost stand now. The water rushing past the side of the boat made her feel nauseous momentarily.

"Listen, I gave you a shot of naloxone. You were drugged. You'll be all right, but you're getting off here."

Tana tried to take all of this in. She couldn't quite follow what he said and didn't understand.

"Knocks what?"

He was moving his arms around her, pulling something over her head and face.

"Hey..."

He stopped and held her by the shoulders. He looked deeply in her eyes.

"Remember my name," he said, holding her head in his hands so she had to look at his face. "Contact anyone and tell them what happened here. My name is Morgan. Remember that."

Tana looked at him. "You're Quiet Man."

He had a pleasant face, not handsome but honest, she thought. His nose had slight bend that told her he'd been in a few hard fights, and a small scar ran down the side on his right cheek. She reached up and tried to touch the scar, but he shook her.

"Don't forget—Morgan. Tell them Pascagoula, BODE warehouse..."

"Brody...Pashmagooola...Pashma..."

Morgan grinned. He turned her around and she was facing the water again.

"Sorry about this."

"Why are..."

He picked her up and threw her over the side of the vessel.

Tana hit the water, submerging several feet before bobbing back up to the surface. She came out of the water gasping and choking.

She was nearly wide awake and alert now. She saw the end of the boat she'd been on pass by, the propellers rumbling in the water only a few feet away.

Tana felt around her shoulders and realized Morgan had slipped a life-preserver over her head. She looked around, trying to get her bearings, and spotted lights on a shoreline. It didn't look far, so she started swimming towards the lights.

The cool water felt good to Tana, refreshing and clearing her head even more.

As she swam, she tried to understand why Morgan helped her. She remembered he said he'd given her naloxone, which may well have saved her life—as if getting her away from the boat hadn't also saved her life.

But he also said something else. Tana tried to remember the last things he'd said: pasta, Brody…?

She remembered now. He said his name was Morgan. He said Pascagoula.

And he said BODE, not "Brody." He was telling Tana what to tell whatever authorities she spoke to, to tell them who he was and what was going on.

As she swam in the river, she turned to see the boat, hoping to see Morgan. She spotted it several hundred yards away. The boat was low and long, and had a structure on the top of it that was boxy—like a Motel 6 on water, just like Bobby said.

The barge. And she had been put in a room with women, so it seemed Bobby was right—they were trafficking women.

Take that and chew on it, Jett Jeanrette!

Morgan was telling her that her suspicion Sandy Basko was involved in it somehow was correct, and that she was in Pascagoula.

Now certain of the purpose of the barge, and the people involved, Tana felt invigorated. She began swimming faster, anxious to get to the shore and a phone to contact someone. The slow moving river was carrying her downstream, but the lights along the shore grew nearer.

Tana was only 50 feet from the shore when she heard the whining sound of a speedboat motor. She could tell the boat was moving upriver, in her direction. She watched as a bright beam of light searched across the water and shoreline.

If they spotted her, she was certain to be killed.

Tana slipped out of the life preserver. She reached out to a branch drifting on the water and tied the life preserver to it.

Then she took a deep breath and dove under the water. In the dark, she could see the wide arcs of the spotlight, and heard the boat drawing nearer.

She would need to break the water's surface to breathe soon. She let her body slowly rise to the surface, even as her lungs began to burn.

Tana fought the instinct to breathe, the instinct that her body was waging in her chest. She forced her arms to move slowly, so no splashing would be visible on the surface.

The light flashed above her, then back after a few seconds.

A third swing of the light, and Tana popped her head out of the water. In a second, she exhaled and took in another deep breath. As soon as she gulped in the fresh air, she used her arms to drop below the surface. She kicked her legs to swim towards the shore again, and moments later, felt the soft touch of the silty river bottom.

Tana rose for another breath. She took notice of the sound of the motorboat, which was moving further away from her upstream.

She swam forward until she could stand in the water.

After making her way ashore, Tana collapsed on the river bank. The events of the night had been disorienting. It all left her feeling exhausted and confused.

As she lay back resting, images and memories began clouding her mind, tumbling over each other, swirling around a central question: what just happened?

She tried to organize her thoughts chronologically, but the pieces wouldn't stay in place: she was kidnapped; she was drugged; she was taken to Sandy Basko; somebody named Morgan threw her from the barge...

It was too much to take in at once. She rested on the ground and pushed it all away.

She needed to get to a phone somewhere. She needed to call police, or the Coast Guard. Someone needs to know about the barge, Morgan, and all of it. She could call Jett.

She heard a quiet splash in the water near her feet, and the sound of wood creaking, making her jump up with a start.

There was a small boat on the river not more than five feet from her, with the dark shadow of a large person—man or woman, Tana couldn't tell—inside the boat, holding dripping oars just above the water.

"The hell's going on?" a deep but womanly voice said. "They looking for you or something?"

27

Tana studied the dark shadowed figure in the boat. She couldn't see her face, but sensed the woman on the boat could see hers, and was studying Tana closely.

"You in some kinda trouble?" The woman said. "Y'all shouldn't be out here."

Tana stood up. She looked around, up and down the river, to see if either the motor boat or barge was in sight.

"I…yes, I need your help." She took a step toward the boat, but as she did, the woman quickly dropped an oar and pushed the boat away.

"I ain't getting in no trouble here," she said. She paused, and Tana could again feel the woman's eyes appraising her. "I seen that boat searching…they looking for you? Why they be looking for a little fish like you?"

Tana suddenly felt overwhelmed. She pushed her wet hair back and twisted around to look behind her. The land was nothing but black brush and trees. She couldn't see any lights nearby.

"I…uh…I need to get some help." She looked at the dark shadow. "Look, that barge that went by has young women on it. They're going to hurt those women. We've got to stop them."

The woman tilted her head, still studying Tana.

"What's your name? My name's Beulah. I'ma fishing here. Catfish."

"Tana, Tana Stone. I'm pleased to meet you, Beulah. Do you have a telephone? Maybe I could call for help?"

Beulah rowed the boat closer to Tana. She chuckled as she pushed the boat forward in the shallow water.

"I got a phone," she said, quietly. "Yeah, I got me a nice, new iPhone."

She lifted the oars out of the water.

"Get yourself in, Miss Tana. I'll take you to a telephone."

Tana pushed the small rowboat backwards into deeper water, then hopped up into it.

"Thank you, Beulah."

Beulah rowed the boat out into the river, joining the flow southward towards the Gulf and the edges of downtown Pascagoula. She rowed with ease and patience, letting the current do most of the work but giving it just enough help to keep the rowboat moving quickly.

Tana was lost in her thoughts for a few minutes, then looked at Beulah. There was more light out in the river, away from the trees that seem to fill the shore and river shallows with dark shadows. Beulah's black skin was tight over her wide face. Her mouth formed a smile, although her large eyes seemed filled with pain and sadness.

Beulah quietly hummed as she rowed and paid little attention to Tana.

"What did you say you were fishing?" Tana asked, looking at Beulah's fishing pole and tin bucket filled with gear.

"Oh, I was hoping for some cats. Usually catch a few catfish on a night like this."

"Catfish are fun fishing, aren't they? Give a good fight when you get one hooked."

"You know about catfishing?" Beulah studied Tana with renewed interest.

"I love fishing. I caught a big old channel catfish in Oklahoma once– –it was 60 pounds and took me an hour to get it to the boat."

Beulah whistled. "Yep, they get pretty big."

She reached out towards Tana, her big hands gripping the oars for the next row. She looked closely at Tana again.

"You kind a pretty little thing to be knowing about big fish, ain't you?"

"I don't know about that, but I grew up fishing. In Missouri."

"Missouri! How about that? I knew you was from somewhere else. So what do you fish in Missouri?"

The two women bonded over their fishing stories. Tana told Beulah about Montana streams, Oklahoma reservoirs; about her work with the St. Louis police before her move to White Sands.

For her part, Beulah told Tana her favorite recipes for the various fish and other aquatic creatures she caught in the Pascagoula.

As they traveled southward, towards the bright dome in the sky from the lights downtown, Tana realized she could see buildings lining the shore. Some were set back from the river; others right on the water, with docks for boats.

An industrial area ahead had several large buildings that Tana could see. She studied them as they passed, noticing the low, windowless warehouses. As her view of one warehouse shifted from the side to the front, she saw a big blue sign on the front: BODE, Inc.

Tana felt the blood drain from her head, and her heart pounding suddenly.

Morgan said to tell police "BODE," and "Pascagoula." She thought he'd meant to tell someone she was in Pascagoula, and that the barge belonged to BODE.

But maybe Morgan meant something else. Maybe the BODE warehouse in Pascagoula was connected to the trafficking operation the barge was conducting. Morgan could be an undercover agent for some law enforcement agency.

Tana noticed a dock jutting out into the water next to the BODE warehouse. Did they use the dock to load and unload people from the barge? What was the warehouse for?

"Beulah, can you take me over to that dock?" She pointed towards the BODE warehouse and dock.

"I can, Miss Tana, but what y'all want to go there for? Ain't no telephone they gonna let you use."

Tana looked at Beulah. "Beulah, I need to go there. But I need you to get to a phone and call the police. Can you do that? Can you call police for me? Tell them you saw me in the river, and I told you that Officer Morgan said to tell them about the BODE warehouse. Mention my name, Tana Stone."

Beulah's face grew concerned.

"Oh, Miss Tana, you sure you want me to do that? You gonna be at that warehouse and the Dear Lord only knows what's to happen."

"Yes, Beulah. It's too important. Remember: Morgan, BODE warehouse Pascagoula, Tana Stone."

"I got it."

Beulah gave a pull on one oar, and the rowboat shifted directions towards the shore.

Tana studied the building. It didn't appear anyone was there, but she was determined to find out how it fit in with the barge.

"Oh, Beulah, I almost forgot. When you call the police, tell them to call White Sands Police, Jett Jeanrette."

"White Sands Police, Jett Jeanrette. You got it, Miss Tana."

The creaky boat drifted up to a ladder at the side of the dock. Tana reached out and grabbed it, scampering up to the dock before Beulah stopped the rowboat's motion by holding the oars against the water.

Tana leaned over the side of the dock.

"Beulah, thank you," she whispered.

Beulah opened her mouth to reply, but Tana ducked out of sight. Beulah rowed her way back to the deeper water and picked up her pace as she moved downstream. As she rowed, she hummed an old tune, then quietly started singing. "Tana say...You call police...They's at the BODE...in Pascagoula...Tana say...Morgan's the man...and Jett Jeanrette..."

Tana squatted on the dock for a moment. The end of the dock was in the dark, but light from the big BODE, Inc. sign illuminated the front of the building and parking lot. Two vehicles sat at the far side of the parking lot, big black SUVs like the ones Tana had seen in White Sands.

Tana also spotted a fenced-in area at the side of the warehouse, and two doors, one in front and one leading to the fenced enclosure. The parking lot appeared to extend around the far side of the warehouse, probably to loading docks in back, she figured.

She moved carefully toward the building. Next to the front door was a window, likely to an office inside the warehouse, but it was dark and when Tana looked, she couldn't see anything inside.

She walked around the enclosed pen, studying the space and the door. The pen extended almost to the edge of the macadam lot, covering everything between the building and the dark woods with only a narrow foot-wide ledge at the outer edge. Tana walked to the back of the pen, and then to the back of the warehouse.

The metal siding across the back of the warehouse was interrupted only by two large loading bays, with the paved lot angled down so trucks could back up to the doors for loading or unloading. Tana climbed up to the loading bay doors and listened closely.

Sounds came from inside the warehouse, movements and footsteps. Tana listened to try to tell how many people were inside. There would be however many came in the SUVs parked out front, of course, but the sounds she heard suggested more. Many more.

She stepped back from the door and studied it. It didn't appear to have any way to open from the outside, so she started back towards the side of the building.

As she turned the corner of the warehouse, she heard the low rumble of a large boat on the river. She looked towards the water. The barge was approaching from the far side of the river.

Tana felt her heart skip a beat. She didn't know how long it would take Beulah to reach a telephone, or how much trouble Beulah might have convincing police to check out her story.

She studied the area behind the warehouse. A path ran from the river past the warehouse and into a thick, dark stand of trees. Maybe it was a path used by local kids who lived nearby; she could use it to get away quickly, if needed.

The barge was close to the dock now, and several men appeared on the deck, standing ready with ropes in hand to jump and tie the craft to the dock.

As Tana watched, the men cinched up the ropes to hold the barge fast to the dock. As soon as they did this, all of the lights on the vessel went out. The motor stopped its rumbling and only the sound of water being pumped out from the side could be heard.

Tana watched. The light from the sign made it easy for her to track their movements. She watched as several men moved about the deck, then a door opened at the side of the barge, a door opposite the door Morgan used to help Tana escape.

Three men stepped out and started toward the warehouse. Tana noticed the first man walked with urgency, his huge muscular body moving towards the warehouse in powerful strides.

In the back of Tana's mind, she knew this was the man who had stood before her when she was first brought to the barge. This was the man in charge of whatever was going on.

Before the man got halfway down the dock, several women stumbled out of the barge door. Several men pushed them roughly onto the dock, and two men with guns who had taken positions on the dock pointed towards the warehouse.

Tana watched as more women and girls followed out of the barge. They were dressed in ordinary clothes, but stumbled and cowered as they passed men. Some appeared Asian; some Hispanic; some European.

Twenty-three women came out of the barge. Tana was stunned—a mass trafficking operation was underway. She still didn't know exactly how White Sands tied into it, but it did.

A few of the men led the women to the front of the pen area, then roughly pushed inside. They huddled around, and several drifted towards the back of the pen. When they spotted Tana, they simply looked at her with blank faces and stood mute.

Tana listen to the men at the front talking. The big man was directing one of the others to "load up for Galveston."

Tana watched as several men turned and disappeared around the side of the warehouse. The big man stood talking to one of the others, looking over the women in the pen. At one point, a gap opened in the crowd and Tana found herself suddenly looking directly at the big man.

He shifted his gaze, and for a second locked eyes with her. Tana's heart stopped, but if he recognized anything when he saw her, he didn't do anything to indicate he had. Maybe he couldn't tell she wasn't with the others inside the fenced area. He continued his scan of the crowd, then turned and walked towards the warehouse door.

If they were loading people to ship to Texas, Tana knew she had to do something, and she had to act fast. She stepped around the back of the warehouse to gather her thoughts, then swiftly moved into action.

She jumped down and made her way to the path she'd spotted before, turning towards the river bank. There, she carefully worked her way to the dock, using the shadows to hide.

Beneath the dock, she slipped into the water and moved quietly to the ladder. She climbed back up, peering carefully over the dock quickly to check for any guards on the dock or barge.

The barge rocked gently in the water, just a few feet from the ladder. Tana worried the huge vessel could shift and smash her against the dock, so she scrambled as fast as she could up the ladder and onto the deck of the barge.

She ran in a crouching position to the rear of the barge superstructure, where a door led to the engine room and other utility areas of the barge. If the barge had lower decks, she might be able open the seacocks, flooding the hull with water to scuttle the boat.

But on a barge, there are no lower decks. Only a wide, flat floating hull with a structure built upon it.

She wouldn't be able to scuttle it, so she needed to find another way to prevent the barge from moving.

Tana searched anxiously around the rear section. She hoped to find a room filled with generators for electrical power for the cabins and living sections of the barge that she could sabotaged. Or perhaps she could damage controls in the engine room.

Tana heard voices outside and quickly slipped inside the generator room. She heard two or three guards outside the room.

They were checking around the barge, and after a moment, continued on. Tana stepped towards the door when she noticed a large tank for the generator fuel, likely gasoline or diesel fuel. The tank had a drain plug on the bottom of the tank, and she got an idea.

She grabbed a wrench from a tool box and forced open the drain valve. She let fuel run onto the floor, then she put a large can beneath the valve and filled it with the fuel.

She carefully opened the door and took a peek outside. No one was in sight, and the barge was quiet, so she stepped out of the generator room and into the engine room next to it.

Her idea was to pour the fuel around the engine room and start a fire. While she had the fuel, she realized she didn't have any way to light it.

She looked around the room hoping to see matches or a cigarette lighter, but nothing helpful was in sight.

Time was running out and Tana knew she only had a few minutes to act before getting caught. She began pouring the fuel, dumping it around the control panels in the room. As she moved around pouring the liquid, she saw a small metal box affixed to the wall next to the door.

She opened it. Inside, she found a flare gun and two flares.

She grabbed the gun and flares and stepped to the edge of the barge. She loaded the flare gun and fired it at the engine room.

The bright flare zipped through the doorway and across the engine room. She saw the flare flash around the room before getting stuck behind the huge block of the engine.

But the fuel on the floor didn't ignite. Did she not let out enough fuel to ignite? If it was diesel fuel, could she even ignite it with a flare?

Tana reloaded the flare gun and fired again, this time pointing the gun at the wet floor in the generator room. She squeezed the trigger and another flash sped into the room.

Just as it zipped across the floor, the fuel ignited in huge blue and yellow flame.

Tana immediately jumped into the water and swam back under the dock. While under the water, she heard a huge explosion above—the storage tank must have ignited. The barge was now disabled.

While a dozen men ran towards the barge overhead, Tana stepped out of the water under the dock.

28

Tana watched flames billow out the back of the barge. Several men frantically tried to put out the fire, while others ran inside the cabin section.

She was at the back of the warehouse again, able to keep an eye on the men on the barge without being seen.

A few minutes later, she stood in horror as men dragged another dozen women from somewhere inside the barge. This group differed from the first group taken from the barge—they were younger women and girls, some barely teens. They were stumbling and disoriented as they moved from the barge to the dock, and Tana realized in horror that she could have killed them all when she ignited the generator room.

The big man stood at the end of the deck. He had his hands on his hips and was barking orders to the men. He grabbed two men and pointed to the pen. The two guards then began pushing the young women towards the pen.

Tana was watching when she noticed a gap between the rear of the building and the post holding the fence. It wasn't a wide gap, certainly not big enough for the men or even some of the women, but Tana might get a least a few women out through it.

She slipped through the gap and stepped into the pen. She slowly and carefully made her way towards the front of the pen where the women clustered.

She stood behind one of the women and gently tapped her shoulder. When the woman turned, Tana saw she was a middle-aged Asian woman, her eyes filled with worry and fear.

Tana pointed towards the back of the pen, then took a step towards it.

"Follow me," she said and waved her arm for the other to follow her.

She slowly walked backwards. The woman hesitantly took a step to follow her. Another noticed and began inching her way back, also.

Soon the women had spread out in the pen, and most made their way towards the back of the fenced in area.

The guards' attention focused on the fire and they didn't notice. Before long, Tana had ten or more of them safely outside the pen. She pointed to the path below, and the women started climbing down to it before scurrying into the darkness of the trees.

Six older women who weren't able to get through the gap remained behind in the pen. One woman looked sharply at Tana and shooed her away, telling her to get away.

Just as Tana turned to leave, she heard the guards shouting. The six women ran towards the front of the pen as if to block the guards view of the back. Several gunshots rang out and two women fell to the ground.

The others raise their hands and slowly got down on their knees.

Tana and the others were out of sight now, running down the path in the midnight dark of the woods. Here and there, a girl or woman would trip, but the others would help her get back up quickly.

They were all quiet, except for two women engaged in a loud argument in Spanish. Tana pressed her way forward until she caught up to the arguing women.

"What? What's wrong?" she said, grabbing both women's shoulders.

They continued arguing, one woman pointing in the direction they were heading while the other glared at Tana. She seemed angry at Tana.

A young girl stepped up beside Tana.

"She says you ruined her."

"What?" Tana didn't understand. She looked from the girl to the women.

"She wants to go back. She says the men take her to a job. A good job in Iowa."

Tana studied the woman. She was middle-aged, a bit overweight, and not the picture Tana had of the kind of women traffickers moved. The girl fit the bill, but not this angry, older woman.

"I...I don't understand. Those men were going to put you in prostitution or..."

"Not her. She was going to work at a hotel. That's where they take the older women."

Tana didn't know what to think, but she knew they had to keep moving. She gave the two women a push.

"Vamos." She turned to the girl. "Tell her to get moving or she's going to be dead when those guys back there catch up to us."

The girl said something, followed by another angry outburst from the older woman—but she turned and started moving down the path again.

Tana told the girl to tell the women to keep going down the path, that police are on the way but they have to put some distance between themselves and the men from the barge.

The girl turned and started speaking in Spanish to the women. She pointed back towards the warehouse and several heads turned to look back.

The group then moved on. Tana stood watching until they were out of sight in the dark.

She jogged back down the path towards the warehouse. As she approached the end of the trail, she spotted the outlines of three men running towards her, having just started down the path. As she watched, one man tripped and fell. She heard a muffled boom, and a scream. The other men stopped and turned around, going back to check on the third.

He must have shot himself when he tripped, Tana thought, and after a moment, the other two men began running in her direction again.

She looked around at the trees in the night's darkness. Her eyes had adjusted to the low light, and what had been a heavy, black darkness of the woods became a shifting blackness, revealing trees in different levels of night. She saw thinner trees, and the wide trunk of a large tree ahead, just off the path. She stepped toward the tree, then felt around on the ground for a branch or stone she could use as a weapon.

The men were less than thirty feet away, moving quickly and quietly. Tana desperately felt around the ground. Just as the first man neared the tree she was behind, she found a thick stone.

Grabbing the stone, she raised up in the dark, just off the path. The first man ran by.

The second man ran by and Tana swung her arm with the stone. She hit him on the back of the head and he fell to the ground without a sound.

Tana jumped out and grabbed his gun, then stood. She carefully studied the shadows, watching for the man running towards the women. His head was barely visible in the darkness, but the black of his shadowed figure was darker than the black of the trees.

She could see the figure bobbing and cutting as he ran. She followed his movement for a few seconds, then squeezed off a shot.

The shadow she was watching lurched forward, then disappeared.

Without waiting, Tana turned and ran back towards the warehouse. She found the man who had tripped and shot himself lying on the trail, unconscious.

As she got nearer, she saw the flashing lights of police vehicles reflecting off trees on the other side of the warehouse.

And a fire engine siren screamed in the distance.

29

Buzzing from his cell phone on the nightstand woke Jett. He'd driven back to White Sands and fallen on his bed without undressing or even kicking off his shoes.

He stirred slowly, then reached out to grab the phone with his left hand and winced from the sharp pain he felt as soon as he moved his arm. He sat up and reached for the phone again, using his other hand.

"What?"

"I'm calling to speak to Jett Jeanrette," a monotone voice said.

"Speaking." Jett rubbed his eyes trying to clear his head.

"This is Officer Anderson, dispatcher with the Pascagoula Police Department. My chief, Sam Mark, requested I call you to inform you we received a message from someone named 'Tina.'"

"Tina? I don't know anyone named Tina."

He rolled over with the phone still in his hand and nearly drifted back to sleep.

"Wait. Pascagoula?" He sat up quickly.

"Yes, sir."

"Could you mean 'Tana?'"

"I cannot answer that, sir. We received a call from a local resident who reported someone threw this woman into the Pascagoula River."

Jett sat up, wide awake now. "What?"

"She reported something concerning a 'Bodie warehouse,' a barge, and an agent named Morgan."

"I remember that warehouse…"

"Chief Mark is headed to the location. We also received a fire alarm at the warehouse."

Jett ran out of his bedroom, still holding the phone to his ear. He needed to get back to Pascagoula quick.

"Is Tana OK?"

"I can't answer that at this time. We are just now responding to the information."

"Please have Chief Mark call me as soon as possible. Tell him I'm on my way."

Jett felt panicked. He stopped and leaned against the front door of his house, taking deep breaths. He closed his eyes and tried to focus on what the dispatcher just told him.

What was Tana doing in Pascagoula? She had been thrown in the river in Pascagoula. Robert's body had been dumped in the river, too…did this mean they'd killed Tana, too?

Jett's knees buckled. It was that damned barge again and now Jett knew BODE was part of it.

He shook off his confusion and stood. His head clear, he knew what he wanted to do first.

Jett tore through White Sands in his borrowed police cruiser, turning onto BODE Drive by the airport and gunning the engine until he came to the BODE lot entrance. He slammed on the brakes, skidding to a halt before striking the guardhouse.

Two men ran out and stood in front of Jett's car, guns drawn and pointed at him.

"Get me Sandy Basko, NOW!" Jett demanded as he stepped out of the car. "I am here on a police matter and I want to see that son-of-a-bitch right now."

Jett started towards the guards, then thought better of it while he was still outside the property line. The guards looked at each other.

"So who the fuck are you?" one said, with a smirk.

"Jett Jeanrette, chief of police. No one will be leaving this lot until I speak to Basko."

Sirens in the distance alerted the guards that Jett had called for backup. A guard stepped to a phone attached to the outside of the guardhouse and picked it up.

"There's a police chief here wants to talk to Mr. Basko."

The guard listened for a moment. "He's got others coming."

Another pause.

"I don't know what it's about. Is Mr. Basko still onsite?" After listening, the guard hung up the phone.

He turned to Jett. "You stay right there. Mr. Basko will be here soon."

Despite the early hour, Sandy Basko was already at work on the lot. He found the stresses of his business and the state of the oil industry kept him from sleeping most nights, and he'd taken to working eighteen hours or more each day.

It took the golf cart he was driving around his facility more than six minutes to get to the guardhouse at the front, six minutes stressful minutes as Jett faced off against the guards. He rolled up and stopped in front of Jett's car.

"I'm Sandy Basko. What can I do for you, Chief?"

"I'm investigating a report of illegal activity on a barge owned by BODE, Inc., and a warehouse in Pascagoula."

Basko stepped closer to Jett.

"I haven't used that Pascagoula warehouse in years. I don't have any barges here. I think y'all got some wires crossed, son."

Basko watched Jett's reddened and baggy eyes closely. He could see Jett was bordering on complete exhaustion, and it occurred to him that Jett could be having a psychotic episode.

"What have you heard?" Basko said.

Jett explained the call from the Pascagoula dispatcher.

"And I just returned from Pascagoula after identifying the body of one of my men."

Basko looked down and kicked at some gravel at his feet. He turned to his guards.

"Where's Mironoff? He should know about this."

"I didn't see him all night," one of the men said.

"Well, get on the goddamn horn and find him." Basko's face reddened. "Now."

Basko turned back to Jett and placed a hand on his arm. He pulled him aside, looking up at the man towering over him.

"Listen, if you want, we can go check this out right now," Basko said. "I can get you over to Pascagoula in no time. If there's someone using my warehouse, I want to know who it is and what the hell they're doing."

Two White Sands police cars pulled up behind Jett. Daggett and Hancock stepped out of the cars.

"DiCicco's on the way, Chief," Hancock said.

Jett just nodded at them. He turned to Basko. "You don't know what's going on at the warehouse?"

Basko gave him a sheepish look. "On my mother's grave, I do not. That's been excess property for some time—in fact, I've been trying to sell it for four years now."

"And you don't have a barge in the Gulf? An accommodation barge?"

"I do not," Basko said firmly. "I got some in Indonesia, couple in the North Sea. None anywheres near here."

Jett watched Basko carefully. His gut was telling him that Basko was not lying, that he was as surprised as Jett to learn about the warehouse.

"How fast can we get to Pascagoula?"

"I can get my heli pilot going, and we'll go straight to the warehouse. Forty minutes, tops."

"Do it."

Jett told Hancock and Daggett to move their cars so he could back out. He also said they should then block the entrance to the BODE lot, and that they were to prevent anyone from leaving until he contacted them.

Basko was on his phone, ordering his pilot to get up and "get the chopper ready to go to Mississip." He said he would meet the pilot at the pad right away with one other passenger.

He eyed the two guards. "One you sons-a-bitches going to find Mironoff?"

Both men quickly jumped into action, with one going to the guardhouse while the other ran towards the office building.

Basko walked to the passenger side of Jett's car and opened the door.

"You OK to drive to my helipad? You look like you been rode hard and put away wet."

He slipped into the car as easily as he might slip into one of his limousines.

Jett climbed in, dropping his weight onto the seat. He backed the car up and watched Hancock and Daggett moved their cars into position to block the exit.

Basko gave directions to a helipad located next the clubhouse of a country club about 10 miles north of White Sands. Jett drove while Basko carried on a conversation with himself about how much he enjoyed White Sands, and hated Houston.

As they passed the airport, Jett pointed to the huge BODE plane parked by a hangar. "We've been getting complaints about that big plane landing and taking off in the middle of the night," he said. "I'd appreciate it if you'd knock it off."

Basko looked from Jett to the plane.

"You talking about that Antonov? My cargo plane?"

"Yes, I'm talking about your cargo plane. Makes a hell of a racket taking off, and a lot of people around here get bothered. Knock it off."

Basko slapped his knee. "God damn."

Jett turned and looked at him. He didn't expect that response.

"Chief, listen here. It's a cargo plane—what the hell am I going to be shipping in such a big ass plane like that in the middle of the night?"

"Oh, I don't know. Maybe some piping. Or a couple thousand pounds of coke…"

"You talking cocaine?" Basko was stunned.

"Yes, cocaine. Or stolen merchandise, or women, or, shit, I don't know."

Basko sat quietly for a minute.

"I'll be a sun-baked Texas monkey. I've been taken in. I been taken in by that giant asshole."

"Who are you taking about?"

"Mironoff, that son-of-a-bitch Mironoff."

They rode silently for a minute while Basko thought back over the last few months, and his work with Mironoff.

"I hired his security firm about five years ago," Basko said. He was talking like a man who'd never found himself outsmarted before and was just realizing he'd been fooled. "He's a scary son-a-bitch—that's what I liked about him—but he had some good references from business people I knew overseas."

Basko said he'd noticed Mironoff being more aggressive, and less visible, in recent months. He didn't know why, but now it seemed he was spending more time doing "side jobs" than paying attention to Basko's business.

"That also explains why we been running higher than expected costs on transportation."

Basko snorted. "Hell, that son-of-a-bitch can't even fill up the fuel tanks after he's used it…"

They arrived at the private club and pulled around the back of the clubhouse. Basko's pilot was already seated inside a blue AgustaWestland helicopter, the motor starting up as he pressed knobs and switches. The rotors on top of the helicopter began slowly rotating.

Despite his short, round build, Basko hopped up into the helicopter's co-pilot seat without effort. He pointed for Jett to get in the back seat which Jett struggled to do with his injured shoulder. Once in, he slumped down in the seat and stared blankly out the window.

The pilot kicked in the rotors, and in seconds they rose up into the sky, then to the west. Pascagoula was just under 60 miles away by air, but the speedy helicopter only needed 20 minutes before they were over the city and approaching the river.

Jett had fallen into a deep sleep as they flew. In his dreams, he was waving to Tana as the helicopter landed. When he got closer, she suddenly turned and ran away, disappearing behind a huge sand dune. Jett was left standing by himself, confused, holding a book and reciting lines from one of his favorite readings in college, John Clare's "The Secret."

A sudden change in the helicopter's altitude of the helicopter woke Jett and as he opened his eyes, Basko was pointing to a building below where lights of a half dozen police cars and a fire truck flashed in the night. Jett looked at the building, seeing the big BODE, Inc. sign again. Beside the building was some kind of boat, with smoke billowing out of it while a small crowd was gathered in front.

Basko told the pilot to land at the back of the warehouse, where the lot was wider so large trucks can pull into the loading docks. As they came down, Jett looked frantically for Tana.

Jett opened the door and leaped from the helicopter when it was still a few feet from the ground. He ignored the pain from the jolt in his shoulder when he landed, and took off in a sprint around to the front of the building, while Basko cursed and hurriedly stepped out of the helicopter.

As Jett rounded the front of the building, he stopped suddenly.

A group of eight Pascagoula police officers stood behind their cars, each with a shotgun pointing at seven men about twenty feet away poised with their own guns aimed at the police. On the far side of the men, a group of women huddled in fear, and past them, the smoking barge.

Five firefighters stood watching nervously, water dripping from hoses they had ready to spray the barge.

One of the police officers stepped to the side of his car—Jett recognized the bulky frame of Chief Mark.

"You men can stand down. There's no reason you need to get yourselves killed."

The men shifted nervously. At first glance, it would appear they had the upper hand, but the police were ready with shotguns, protected by their cars.

Basko came jogging around the corner of the warehouse and

suddenly stopped.

"Sweet Jesus Palomino!"

Several men looked over at Basko, then nudged the others to also look.

Basko stepped towards them.

"What the hell you boys up to here? Put them guns down before I start kicking asses and taking names."

The men started dropping their guns, and dropping to their knees. Police approached them, handcuffing the men, and began loading them in the waiting cars.

While the firefighters rushed to the barge, Jett ran to the crowd of women. He frantically pushed his way through them, looking for Tana.

He found her at the back of the group, sitting on the pavement.

30

Mironoff watched the helicopter land from the path behind the warehouse. He had noticed the flashing lights of police cars on the river and immediately turned and ran to the back of the building.

From there, he watched police arrive and the stand-off between his men and the police begin. It was Broussard, the man he'd left in charge of the warehouse who then got him to dash to the path Tana used to help the women escape earlier.

Just before ducking into the trees, Mironoff heard the helicopter. He stopped to see who was in it. When he saw a tall man with his left arm in a sling and Sandy Basko jump out of it, he cursed and spat.

This meant the end of everything. The agreements he had to provide workers for hotels and industrial plants throughout the middle of America, for strip clubs from New York to Los Angeles, for overseas oil fields and brothels near military bases, were now nothing but broken promises. Some of them promises to people who wouldn't take kindly to Mironoff's broken assurances.

To watch the barge burn was bad; to have his warehouse, the place where he collected and sorted women, girls, and even some men desperate for work, shut down was a disaster.

He had more than sixty people inside the warehouse readied to distribute; sixty placements already paid for but which Mironoff would not be able to deliver.

He slowly stepped backward on the path, into the still black darkness of the trees, in a daze. He turned and went to the body of one of his men lying on the path. Broussard was removing things from the body, identification, ammunition, a knife, and the money in the dead man's pockets.

Broussard stood.

"Boss, I got a small boat over on the water. We gotta go."

Mironoff stood looking down at the dead man. "I am as dead as this man, now," in a low, cold voice.

"Let's go." Broussard pulled on Mironoff's arm, tugging him off the path and towards the river.

Mironoff tensed and yanked his arm from Broussard's grasp.

"We got to go now, Boss."

"I will find and kill Basko and that woman, that fucking woman."

They turned and began jogging through the brush towards the river, Mironoff mumbling under his breath as they ran.

"I will hunt police man. I will hunt woman. I will kill them and find new location. This is big country. Lots of empty warehouses. Lots of people to sell and people to sell to."

Broussard noted Mironoff's speech had reverted to a mix of accents, some Russian, some a kind of Middle Eastern dialect. He'd heard this before when Mironoff was extremely angry or distressed, like when the girl had called someone from the warehouse just after he'd finished the work preparing it. It was in his coldest, most accented English then that Mironoff told Broussard to "keel bitch."

Broussard grew nervous listening to the rambling curses and threats coming from Mironoff.

The ground soon turned mushy, with water grasses growing in a marshy area. Broussard quickly found the small boat he'd tied up in the marsh to use when he could. He had been supervising the warehouse operation, which once running smoothly, left him some time for boating on the river.

They jumped into the boat, and Broussard turned to take them upriver. Mironoff sat in a seat placed on the front of the boat, arms crossed and a scowling face frozen in anger. They traveled more than 30 minutes without speaking, only the humming of the boat's little outboard motor filling the dawn's air.

"Broussard, we go to White Sands."

"Sure thing, Boss." Broussard wasn't certain how he would get them to White Sands, but he had been thinking of their escape. He planned to land upriver and thought he could then steal a vehicle and drive Mironoff somewhere to get away.

He had friends on the Gulf who could take them to Mexico, or even Venezuela; other friends further north could take him to Washington or Oregon, where they could hide out in the mountain forests while they planned their next move.

Instead, it looked like they will travel back to White Sands while Mironoff plotted.

Broussard guided the boat a few more miles upriver, almost as far as Escambia, before pulling nearer to the shore to look for suitable landing spots. They spotted a newer house on the river that appeared to be someone's weekend get-away lodge. After getting off the boat and pushing it away to float downstream, Broussard walked down the road looking for a car to steal. About a mile away, he found an old blue Ford sedan.

They pulled into White Sands before 8 a.m., and the town was just waking up. Mironoff guided Broussard to a 22-story condominium building on the beach, then told him to get rid of the car in some safe place.

While Broussard was disposing of the Ford, Mironoff went to the condo he'd purchased on the 20th floor in the name of a limited liability company he organized. The LLC ownership hid his involvement, and he had never told anyone about it. Basko knew nothing of his real business, Mironoff thought.

Mironoff figured this would give them some safety while he worked on his plan for revenge.

Inside, he poured a large tumbler of vodka and stepped onto the balcony. A chilling breeze blew in off the Gulf, but Mironoff didn't mind. The vodka warmed him and fueled his thinking.

He used an address in Perdido on his contract with BODE, so anyone looking for him would focus investigations there. He could use Broussard as his eyes and ears, and find out how he could get rid of Basko, the woman, and the cop.

He didn't know who the woman he'd seen in Pascagoula, the one who had disrupted everything, was, nor did he know how to find her. He figured she was police or FBI or something like that, but which agency she worked for he couldn't be sure. And he didn't care. She wouldn't be the first federal agent to die after interfering in his plans.

When Broussard returned three hours later, Mironoff was ready with his plan.

31

Wind blew a crumbled paper past headstones and graves, catching Tana's eyes and distracting her from Robert's funeral underway.

Jett and the entire White Sands Police Department stood behind the pastor, on the opposite side of the silver casket holding Robert Gulliford's body.

The pastor began speaking, but she didn't hear much of what he said.

She was again engaged in an internal dialogue, or diagnosis, or discourse, or whatever you want to call it when she shut out everything around her and let herself get lost in her own thoughts. If she had PTSD before all this began, what did she have now? Is there such a thing as "extra-post traumatic stress" or "super-traumatic stress?" She felt lost in a fog of names for her new self-diagnosis.

After the service, people began walking back to their cars. Tana remained, staring blankly at the grave, oblivious to the conversations and condolences among the people around her.

Tana's mind filled with clouds of thoughts and words, images of Robert, the sight of the paper rolling in the wind. She suddenly remembered balaclavas, the last thing she'd spoken to him about.

Why was she so fixated on balaclavas then? Why hadn't she asked him more about what he was doing? More about the barge he saw and that she later destroyed after the people on it tried to destroy her?

She almost jumped when the thought of balaclavas brought to mind the videos she'd watched. It dawned on her that robbers in the videos wore the same clothing as the men at the warehouse in Pascagoula. She needed to check, but she felt certain the men's shirts had a symbol on them identical to the shirts worn by men on the barge and at the warehouse—if she could see the shirts well enough on the camera recordings.

She was still working through these connections, when Jett stepped up to her. He waited patiently for a moment, then when she didn't notice him, gently touched her shoulder. She blinked her eyes, then turned towards Jett.

"Jett, I…" She hadn't seen him since the warehouse in Pascagoula, almost a week ago. She looked at his uniform, crisp and starched—except for the white sling holding his still-healing left arm. "I was…the robberies…the guys in balaclavas…same as at Pascagoula."

Jett watched her as she mumbled her thoughts. He waited for her to finish before speaking.

"I know," he said. "Some of the guards have been cooperative. We found out those robberies were supply runs…for feminine products. They figured they couldn't just go into stores and buy large quantities without drawing attention, so they used the robbery as a distraction."

"Oh…" This made sense, Tana thought. That's what the second man at each robbery was doing when they disappeared from view of the security cameras.

A silence grew between them. Jett shifted nervously.

"Tana, how are you?"

Tana looked down and nervously picked at fabric pilling on the black sweater she'd pulled on for the funeral. "I don't know, Jett. It's been tough."

"I hear that." Jett guided her away from a small group of people standing nearby. "I've been wanting to talk to you. We never had a chance to talk about what happened. To us. Before, I mean."

"Uh-huh." Tana's mind was still somewhere else, Jett decided.

"I read the report about what had happened to you on the barge. I…I can't believe it."

Tana still tugged on the pilling on her sweater.

"Could we, I mean, I'd like to…"

She stepped back and looked up at Jett, as if seeing him for the first time in his uniform.

"Look at you! You clean up pretty nicely, you know that?"

Jett grinned. "Thanks. Let's have dinner."

Her face dropped. "What?"

"Dinner. You and me. We need to talk."

"Oh, Jett, no. I don't think I'm ready for us to…"

"Tana, I understand. I know I was coming on too strong before.

That's why you pushed me away."

Tana looked up at Jett, searching his face. Did she push him away? She felt her anger rising.

"The thing is, I really enjoy your company. The way you can just be still, it…well, it calms me. I don't know what goes on in your head all the time, but it's OK. I just really want…"

He tried to find his words. He had watched her through the service, feeling separated from everyone present and longing for Tana's company. He didn't hear a word said during the service as he planned out what he wanted to say to her.

But Tana had a way about her that always screwed up his thinking. He wanted to be near her, to be around her more, to love her, but something always seemed to get between them, and he wasn't sure what it was.

"Jett, I don't think I'm in a good place right now. I have enjoyed being around you, too, but, I'm just…just…"

She struggled the find the right word, then spit out the closest she could find. "Screwed up."

Jett opened his mouth to reply, then stopped, unsure of what he needed to do. He had to keep Tana talking to him, keep the door open to building on their relationship.

As he stammered trying to find the words he wanted to use, a thin, casually-dressed man stepped up at his side.

"I apologize for interrupting, but are you Chief Jeanrette?"

"Yes. What can I do for you?"

"Oh, I just wanted to shake your hand, and to say thank you." The man stuck out his hand for Jett to shake. "I knew Officer Gulliford, and it's just such a terrible thing."

"Thank you," Jett said, studying the man's face and demeanor. "It is. How did you know Robert?"

"We used to play pool up in Bougainville. Used to go every Saturday, and he'd be there. Lost a lot of games to him—and a lot of money."

"And what is your name?"

Tana noticed the man's eyes tighten just a little.

"Name's Chad Broussard, chief."

Tana noticed Jett's odd expression. "Nice to meet you, Mr. Broussard."

Broussard smiled at Tana and took a step back from them. "Miss," he said to her, gesturing as if tipping a hat. They watched him walk away.

"As I was saying, Jett, I'm not sure this is a good timed for us…"

Jett was still watching Broussard walking away. "What's the matter?"

"Something wrong about that guy."

"Why do you say that?"

Jett looked at Tana. "Bobby was a terrible pool player. Hated the game. I don't believe he would ever went to Bougainville to play pool."

***

Broussard walked to his car, then pulled out his cell phone and dialed Mironoff.

"Did you get the picture?"

"Yes," Mironoff sneered. "Good work."

"Is that the woman?"

"It is, indeed."

"They seemed in the middle of a personal conversation."

"Perfect. We may only need one stone. Come back to the condo."

Broussard started up the car and drove down the lane snaking its way through the cemetery. Jett watched the car passing and took note of the license plate. There was something not right about this man Broussard.

32

Jett pestered Tana to meet for dinner for a few days before Tana finally relented. They made plans to go to a new Creole restaurant on Mobile Bay for dinner.

Jett picked Tana up in his old Chevy Blazer. They chatted easily on the way to the restaurant and through the meal.

Tana wanted to keep the conversation light, but during a lull in the conversation, she felt she needed to apologize too Jett.

"I've been a pain in the butt, haven't I?" she said. "I know I hurt you before, but I wasn't…"

She struggled to find the words. "I wasn't feeling well. Looking back, I was pretty messed up when I moved here."

Jett sat silently, waiting to see if she had more she wanted to say.

"How are you doing now?" he asked after a moment.

Tana sat quietly for a minute before answering, then suddenly brightened.

"Did you know I redecorated my living room?" she laughed. "Of course, you don't. I haven't really talked to you in a couple of months."

She told Jett how she had tried to copy the living room from the Pinterest page, but that once she'd done it, she hated it.

"So I bought a new sofa and table, some window shades, and a couple gallons of paint after the funeral. Then gave away the *other* new sofa and table. Job done, but, yeah, I'd say that still counts as a crazy thing to do."

She paused, gathering her thoughts. "So, I'm still working through some things."

Jett saw she had more to say, and he waited for her to finish.

"I wasn't always like this, getting these weird blackouts when I'm thinking about something. Wasn't always so…so damned anxious about…about everything."

"I think you've done remarkably well here. I really can't believe after all you've been through—even what you went through just last week."

"All this time, I thought I was dealing with dad's murder, and my screw-up at work." She took a sip from her glass of wine. "But I've been feeling lately like there's something else. Something besides all that."

"What do you mean? Losing your dad that way must have been very traumatic—and I always knew you weren't really responsible for his murder."

A tear rolled down Tana's cheek. As she wiped it away, she suddenly felt a heaviness fall on her, a crushing weight that until recently seemed to strike her with greater urgency and frequency.

"Thank you, Jett." She leaned forward and looked intently at Jett. "I have this feeling of something terribly wrong, that something else happened."

"Why do you say that?"

"I don't know, really." Her hands fidgeted on the table, and she tried to hide her nervousness by moving her hands to her sides. "I keep thinking…or imagining…someone dying suddenly, someone not my dad."

Jett sighed. "Tana, let's recount your last year: your father was murdered during a burglary; you quit your job of what? Twenty-some years; you moved to White Sands; you were attacked by a killer in your own home—who you then killed."

He paused and took a breath before continuing.

"And just a couple of weeks ago, you were kidnapped, drugged…who knows what would have happened if Morgan hadn't been able to help save you."

Jett reached for her hand. "I think you're pretty amazing, Tana. I really do."

Tana felt her cheeks redden and she turned to watch the calm water on the bay.

"Thank you, Jett, but I'm worried. No one knows what happened to Mironoff, and frankly, he scared me."

"We'll find him. There are too many agencies searching for him."

"Jett, you don't understand. This man is dangerous in a way I've never seen before. I've been around killers, pedophiles, predators, con men, cartel gangs, you name it, we saw it St. Louis. But this guy? He's a whole other level."

Jett studied her closely. Her tone had changed. There was something she hadn't told him.

"When they drugged me, and took me on that barge, I saw him. Up close." Tana shivered at the thought. "Even as high as I was, I could feel…cold…it was like he had no soul whatsoever."

She was thinking about that moment when Mironoff stood in front of her, appraising her and determining her fate.

"He was inhuman—even not animal. He made a serial killer like Joey Beaumont seem like a Scout…"

She drifted off, staring into the last of the wine in her glass.

"They won't catch him. Guys like that don't get caught."

Jett reached for her hand.

"Tana, Mironoff is probably somewhere in South America or Asia or God knows where. He's not going to pop up here where we know about him."

He waited while she seemed to think about Mironoff, although he could tell she wasn't completely convinced. Time to change the subject.

"So you redecorated, huh? That sounds like a bit of a breakthrough."

"Yeah, I guess."

"It was difficult, though, wasn't it?"

"I thought I could be like a normal person and have a room that looked like a normal person's room…but I guess I'm not normal."

She finished the wine in a quick swallow.

"I just seem to get screwy when things are too organized, too neat. I think that's my big problem."

"It makes you feel confined and nervous?"

"Yeah, that sums it up."

Jett chuckled. "I need to show you my office at home—I've got twenty years of books I plan to read stacked up by my desk, which is covered with the bills I've gotten since about 2001 when I set everything up on automatic payment."

He saw a look of concern cross Tana's face. "Oh, I keep my kitchen clean—I never use it, so there's no roaches or a sink full of last week's dinner plates. It's just my office. Whenever I clean it, I just can't sit still in it. Does that happen to you?"

"It does, sometimes," Tana said with a laugh. The mood lightened for a moment, but the smile on Tana's face quickly faded. "Sometimes,

163

I get these terrible things going around in my head, especially if there's nothing out of place or just a little off. I guess that's what makes me good at what I do—I'm naturally drawn to the things that are out of place, that don't add up. My head just focuses on those things."

Jett nodded in understanding, but didn't interrupt her.

"And lately, when I've got a lot of things in mind—like when I was looking at those robberies along the Interstate—I keep getting these weird thoughts about someone, like I'm seeing someone die or get killed or something. It's got me thinking a lot about what's happened in the past."

She paused before adding, "Jett, do you think it could be something I'd forgotten from my police work? Maybe something I witnessed on the job?"

"I don't know, Tana. I suppose it could be."

They fell quiet, and after a minute, the restaurant server approached. Jett signaled for the bill, then settled up.

As they stood to leave, Jett wrapped an arm around Tana. He was careful not to hold her too tightly just yet. He was afraid it would cause her to panic as it had the last time they went out to dinner.

At the door, he stepped to push the door open for Tana, but she suddenly stopped.

"Oh, I left my phone on the table." She turned to go back. "You go ahead, I'll be right there."

Jett walked out to the Blazer in the parking lot and climbed in. His arm was no longer confined in a sling, but his damaged shoulder was still weak, and climbing up into the four-wheel-drive vehicle was still a painful and difficult proposition.

He looked up to see Tana walking out of the restaurant. How complex she was, so small but so strong, he thought. He took in her long hair, a mahogany wave rolling down past her shoulders; her eyes that burned into him like no one else's ever had. He was more certain than ever that he would do whatever it took to make Tana part of his life. A big part of his life.

He smiled and turned the key to start the Blazer.

A second later, a flash and explosion lifted the Blazer several inches off the ground. Tana, walking towards the vehicle, was thrown to the ground, as the blast sent flames through the truck and a wave of heat that burned Tana's face and arms even though she was still twenty feet away.

Stunned, Tana looked up. Flames engulfed the Blazer, black smoke billowing out as tires melted. She stood uneasily, her legs shaking, just as a crowd of people rushed from inside the restaurant.

"Michael!" she screamed.

33

Boussard watched the flames billowing from under Jett's Blazer from a parking lot next to the restaurant. He had seen Jett get in the vehicle and saw Tana on the other side of the vehicle before dialing the number on his cell phone to trigger a detonator for the explosive device he'd placed underneath the vehicle.

The explosion was even bigger than expected, destroying the Blazer completely and undoubtedly killing the driver. Broussard felt confident the woman was too close to the truck not to have also been killed and was pleased with his work.

Satisfied he'd completed his task, he pulled out of the parking lot and heading back to Mironoff's condo. When he arrived, Mironoff was on a small balcony at the front of the building, watching smoke from Jett's incinerated Chevy rising a mile away to the east.

He turned and greeted Broussard with a wide smile. "It's done?"

"Yes. I followed them to a restaurant and slipped the bomb under the guy's Blazer while they were inside."

"And you saw them get in?"

"I did, Boss. They're dead."

"One stone, two birds."

Mironoff stepped from the window and walked to a bar adjoining the big condo's living room. He grabbed a bottle of Stoli Elite from the shelf behind the bar and two tumblers. He filled both, then held one towards Broussard.

Broussard looked at the clear liquid. "Got any whiskey?"

"For celebration? Whiskey? No, I think we have Stolichnaya." Misonoff drained the full glass, and pushed the other towards Broussard.

"I'd really rather a whiskey…"

Mironoff's eyes narrowed. "No. I don't have whiskey. Maybe you'd like me to piss in glass for you?"

Broussard's face flushed. Just a minute ago Mironoff was happy, elated even, at the job he'd done. Now, the accent was back and he acted like a petulant child because Broussard preferred whiskey over vodka.

"Take the Stoli and drink it," Mironoff commanded. "Now, or I throw you off the balcony."

He gave Broussard a deadly smile.

Broussard reached for the tumbler and drank it. He stared at Mironoff as he did, hoping to convince Mironoff that all was well, that he drank the vodka in celebration with Mironoff.

"What are you going to do about Basko?"

Mironoff poured another glass of vodka and walked to the balcony. He leaned over the railing, taking in the wide expanse of the Gulf. The distant horizon was growing darker as the sun set, and as it did most evenings, held a cover of clouds just above.

Broussard followed, wishing he could have that whiskey. He knew Mironoff had several whiskies in his bar—hell, he'd bought two of them last week. But that's the way the man was.

Broussard leaned against the balcony railing. He looked down and watched the waves rolling up to the beach. Several black rays glided through the water, gently waving their wings to move.

Mironoff twisted towards him, still holding his glass of Stoli.

"I'm working on plans for Basko." He took a deep drink. "Why so hard for you to drink with me?"

Broussard looked at Mironoff in shock. "But…I did. We did celebrate."

"I made you," Mironoff sneered. "I made you drink it instead of piss-water whiskey. I feel I twisted your arm for top-shelf vodka. What sense does this make?"

For a moment, they were locked in a stare. Then, something hit Broussard the side of his head, flashes danced in his vision. He was dazed. He hadn't seen Mironoff swing his arm and the speed at which Mironoff struck him with the glass was frightening.

His head spun dizzily and he tried to regain control over his thoughts and movements.

But in that brief moment, Mironoff grabbed Broussard by his belt and his shoulder. Broussard was aware that Mironoff had lifted him up, lifted him like he'd lift a child. His scrambled senses felt movement, of his view changing directions, suddenly seeing the balcony sideways, then the darkening evening sky.

Mironoff pitched him over the balcony railing. Without watching, he turned and went back into the condo.

A minute later, he emerged from the condo dressed in a blue Adidas track suit. He calmly walked to a sidewalk alongside Gulf Highway, and began jogging, looking like a dozen other people out for an evening jog.

He had a backpack with him filled with a few clothes and $80,000 cash.

Six miles down the road, thirty minutes' time jogging, was another condo. One with the materials he needed to take care of Basko.

34

An EMT on the ambulance held Tana down while he cinched a strap across her waist. He struggled to keep her from getting off the gurney as she twisted and turned in an effort to get up. Sirens outside the vehicle scolded vehicles to make way for the vehicle, and the ambulance sped down the road on the way to the medical center.

"Oh, God, no. No!" Tana kicked and fought against the restraints, but they were just tight enough to keep her from hurting the EMT or herself. The EMT watched her as he drew a syringe with a sedative. He put the vial containing the drug down, then jabbed the needle into Tana's arm.

She stilled and fell quiet. They'd covered the burns on her face and arms with Kling dressing, ointment oozing out the sides of the gauzy bandages.

"What the hell was she going on about?" the ambulance driver asked.

"I don't know. Must be trauma."

"She was with the police chief, right?"

"That's what I was told."

"But his name is Jett…why was she crying 'Michael?'"

"I don't know. Like I said, I guess she's traumatized."

"No shit, seeing someone killed like that."

At the hospital, nurses and several doctors examined Tana's burns more carefully. She had second-degree burns on a spot on her left forearm and another on her right cheek which the staff tenderly redressed.

When finished, Tana stood and walked to the emergency room exit in a daze. As she stepped through the exit door, a tall red-headed woman in her mid-40s stopped her.

"Ms. Stone?" Tana gave the woman an empty look. "My name is Kris Linicum, ABI Major Crimes. I understand you were with Jett this evening."

Tana blinked a few times and furrowed her eyebrows as she worked to think through everything that had just happened. "Jett? Yes, we had dinner."

She looked around anxiously. "Where is he? Did he get burned badly?"

Kris placed a hand on Tana's arm and pulled her over to a group of chairs in the waiting room. They sat down.

"Ms. Stone, Jett was killed in the explosion that caused your burns."

"But he'll be..."

Kris waited patiently as her words seeped through Tana's clouded mind. Tana started crying. "It's pretty clear this was an assassination. We think you were also targeted."

She paused again, carefully watching Tana digest each piece of information.

"I need to know what you remember."

Another pause.

"What happened, Tana? Can you tell me what you remember?"

Tana thought hard. They were sitting at the table in the restaurant. She remembered looking out at the bay. They are talking about his office. They walked to the door.

"I left my phone on the table..." Tana said weakly.

"OK."

"I went to get it and Jett went to his truck."

"And then?"

"I came out, and it just...oh, God. It just exploded."

Kris waited another minute before continuing. "Tana, several witnesses said you screamed 'Michael.' Do you know why you did that? Did you see someone you knew, someone named Michael? Maybe the person who killed Jett..."

"Michael?" Her eyes suddenly widened. "I...I can't...oh...oh, God..."

She swooned and collapsed in the chair, nearly slipping to the floor before Kris caught ahold of her and held her up.

Kris called for help and two nurses came with a stretcher to take Tana back into one of the curtained bays. She took a chair in a corner of the little curtained room and waited for Tana to recover.

Tana opened her eyes after a few minutes. She rolled her eyes to look around the room, momentarily uncertain of where she was. Kris jumped up and stepped to the side of the bed.

Before Kris could say anything, Tana began sobbing. She rolled onto her side, and curled up, fists in her eyes to block out the world.

"Tana, I need to know if you saw anything that will help us," she said in a calming low tone. "Is this Michael connected to what happened to Jett?"

Tana sniffed and eventually rolled back to look at Kris. "No," she said. Tears flooded her eyes, and she wiped at the tears with shaking hands. "No, Michael was my husband."

Kris took Tana's hand. She didn't understand—no one mentioned Tana had husband. Why was she out with Jett? Didn't one of the White Sands officers say they were dating or something when Kris called after hearing Jett was killed? "No one told me you're married."

Tana sat up. Her face was pale and her eyes reddened. She struggled to control her breathing, with every other breath interrupted by a gasping sob. "It was…a while ago."

"Tana, do you remember seeing anything tonight that might help us? We need to find the people responsible for Jett's death."

Tana closed her eyes and worked to regain control over her emotions. She cleared her head, then thought back over the seconds just after the blast.

"A car. I saw a car driving away at the same time." She focused her eyes on the bed's footboard and focused her mind on the car. "I've seen it before, it's an old car but I saw it…"

She looked up at Kris. "I saw the same car last week at Robert's funeral. Some guy who talked to Jett drove away in it."

"Who was this guy? What was his name?"

Tana tried to think. She hadn't really been paying too much attention to the brief conversation Jett had with the man, but she remembered something about the man troubled Jett.

"Jett thought there was something off with the guy. He's tall, almost as tall as Jett, and thin. Twenties, I think. He said his name, but I can't…"

Tana tried to find the right name. She remembered it started with "b," but what was it?

"Buss…Bust…Brewster? No, not that. Something like Brewster, though."

Kris sat down. "Broussard?"

"Yes! Broussard."

Kris began filling Tana with the investigation into the warehouse and barge operation that got Robert killed, much of it information Jett had already told her.

"You might remember someone at the FBI I've been working with, Donald Morgan?"

"Jett told me he was on the barge," Tana said flatly.

"Yes, he was undercover in a trafficking operation we knew was working in the area, we just didn't know how it was operating."

Kris then described the setup inside the warehouse that Tana helped break up, and how a man named Atlas Mironoff ran the operation.

"I saw Mironoff. He's a scary one."

"Oh, yeah, you could say that," Kris said. "From what we know, he's been operating in a number of countries around the world, doing anything and everything from mercenary work for dictators, to industrial espionage, drug running, and of course, trafficking. He had set up an organized, industrial-scale human trafficking operation."

She paused for a moment before continuing.

"Broussard was his right-hand man."

"Oh my God." The connections Mironoff's operation had to so many recent events surprised Tana. "Where's Broussard now?"

"He's poolside at one of the condos on the beach," Kris said. "Seems to have fallen from one of the upper-floor balconies a little while ago."

"And Mironoff?"

Kris raised an eyebrow.

"Oh. Oh, shit."

"Yes. Oh, shit."

"The women on the barge, some of them were upset when I got them away. I remember one woman was really mad because she said she was losing a good job. I thought most would be used as sex workers, but this woman said something about a hotel job."

"Not surprising," Kris said. "I can show you statistics that only about half of the women trafficked in this country are placed in any of the sex trades. Another ten percent are headed for hotels and motels, so your woman was probably talking about that."

"Some guards told us Mironoff set up the warehouse as a 'holding' spot to divide up and send off people he was trafficking," she continued. "He had people coming in from across the country, from other countries...it was incredible."

"But he's still out there?"

"Yes, unfortunately."

"Am I in danger?"

Kris took a deep breath. "I don't know. He may think you were killed with Jett. He may know otherwise, though."

Tana rested and closed her eyes. Kris saw another tear forming in the corner of her eye.

"Tell me about Michael."

Tana rolled her head and looked at Kris.

"We met in college, at Columbia. Columbia, Missouri, not the university. We both majored in criminal justice, but he went to law school after."

Tana inhaled deeply, then continued.

"We kinda lost track of each other for a few years, but I saw him in court one day when I was in to testify." She looked at Kris. "He wasn't working the case I was testifying for, just to be clear…things might have gone differently if he had been, but, anyway, we started dating and well, got married."

Tana stopped talking. Kris knew she was coming to the hard part and was gathering whatever strength she had left to say it.

"We were out one night and started arguing over something…I think it was a case he was working on, but I'm really not sure."

Tana reached for a Kleenex box on the table next to her bed. "We were in the car, I remember. He started to get out of the car and as I turned to him, someone…a bang…he just fell..."

Tana began sobbing uncontrollably again and Kris stood. She stroked Tana's arm trying to comfort her and let Tana sob as much as she needed. A nurse entered the room, holding a clipboard.

"I need to check…"

"Get out. Get the fuck out now!" Kris said, scaring the nurse away. She turned her attention back to Tana. "That must have been horrible, Tana. And then with your father getting murdered…"

Tana opened her eyes and sat up.

"That was…that happened…it was only two days later…" Tana's memories of Michael's death had been buried behind her father's murder; the shock of the two events so close together bunched up into one black hole in her memory. She'd built a wall to hide the hardest and most painful part of it all, putting it away behind another almost as painful.

And ever since, she had grieved for John Stone, her father, and not for Michael James, her husband. Without even realizing what she had done, she locked away all of her memories of the ten years she and Michael were married. She all but forgot about their shared moments, and her love for Michael—and his love for her.

It was all bricked up in her mind she couldn't see behind it, a wall of protection, or maybe a wall of shock.

"Oh, my God," Tana whispered. "I've been blocking these memories of Michael, but it was just hidden behind my father's death. All this time."

Kris studied Tana. My God, what this woman has been through, she thought. She wanted to stay and help Tana get home, get to know her better, but she needed to get back to Mobile and the ongoing hunt for Atlas Mironoff.

"Tana, I don't know how you're going to get through the next few days," she said. "But if you need to talk, or if there's something you need me to do, just call me. OK?"

She tucked one of her Bureau of Investigation cards under Tana's phone on the table.

Tana nodded at her, then rolled onto her side.

35

Waves rolled up the beach, then fell back into the Gulf, chased by plovers and sandpipers along the way. Tana walked along, even though she'd dressed to run this morning as she did every other day.

But she felt quieter today and walking fit her mood better. She carefully stepped over jellyfish scattered along the shore, and once, a piece of driftwood with pink and brown striations. She came across a large conch shell washed up next to a fat jellyfish and stopped to pick it up.

The shell was almost complete but missing a section at the top. She turned it over in her hands, studying the fracture. Just as suddenly as a wave from the Gulf, a wave of grief washed over her. She wanted to scream and cry, but held herself still for a moment, waiting for the wave to recede.

When it did, she dropped the shell and continued down the waterline.

The last week had been like this, drifting through days and letting waves of emotion wash over her. For the most part, just doing that had felt right, like there was no way or reason to fight it—it would be as useless as trying to hold back the waves of the Gulf.

As she went through the days, a smell, a color, or a thought from who knows where would suddenly wash over and flood her with emotion. Sometimes, she would have to fight to keep from bursting into tears, even though she didn't always win the fight.

But somehow, she felt clearer than she had in a long time. The morning sunlight seemed brighter, and the heaviness that had weighed on her for the last year lifted.

Soon after she got home from the hospital, she had taken a thick notebook out of a basket next to the new table and began writing in it.

At first, she just wrote words, words that randomly came to mind. Not in sentences, or sensible order, just words. But soon she found she was writing down memories of things she'd long ago forgotten, or never even thought about.

She wrote about the time she and Michael visited his family in Pensacola and came to White Sands for a romantic weekend. How the rays swam around their tangled legs as they embraced in the warm, salt water.

She wrote about the time her father caught a hook in his thumb when they were high in the mountains in Montana and had to drive three hours to get to a doctor to remove it.

She wrote about how her mother smelled of lilacs and lavender, and how she always seemed surrounded by the colors of those flowers.

And after writing stories like these for hours, she wrote how she had wronged Jett, how she had panicked when he held her closely one night after dinner. She screamed at him, slapped him, told him to never call her again.

And she wrote how she regretted it as soon as she'd done it.

She kept writing over the next few days, spewing forth her pent-up thoughts and memories. Each filled page of the notebook left her feeling more in control of herself. Each time she wrote down one long-forgotten memory, another would soon come to mind.

She wished she'd loved Jett like she knew he loved her. But she hadn't and now it was too late.

All she had now were handfuls of memories that felt like she was clutching grains of sand, slipping through her fingers. The friction of the slipping grains was growing hotter, building in intensity.

She was alone again, sitting at the beat-up table she used as a desk. There wasn't a case folder on it now, and she wasn't finding her mind getting tied up in endless cycles around random words or ideas.

Instead, she found she could choose what she wanted to focus her thoughts on, and once chosen, she could concentrate without becoming unmoored from reality in front of her. She could analyze more easily, but still let her mind wander when she wanted.

She opened her notebook once again, flipping through the pages to find a blank one. After pressing the paper to keep it flat and still, she lifted a pencil from the holder on the desk next to the lamp she bought that she'd seen featured on Pinterest.

Tana began writing, but this time, she wasn't recording memories, or impressions from her childhood, or her emotional responses to events.

She wrote two words, then sat back to let her mind wander and do its work to find ideas and linkages. She looked down at the words she'd written on the page: *Who is Atlas Mironoff?*